ALSO BY LOIS GOULD

Subject to Change

La Presidenta

Not Responsible for Personal Articles
(essays)

A Sea-Change

Final Analysis

Necessary Objects

Such Good Friends

For Children

X: A Fabulous Child's Story

Q: A Perfect Child's Story

MEDUSA'S GIFT

MEDUSA'S GIFT

by

LOIS GOULD

Alfred A. Knopf New York 1991

THIS IS A BORZOI BOOK
PUBLISHED BY ALFRED A. KNOPF, INC.

 Published in the United States by Alfred A. Knopf, Inc., New York, and simultaneously in Canada by Random House of Canada Limited, Toronto. Distributed by Random House, Inc., New York.

ISBN 0-394-58229-2
LC 91-53915

Manufactured in the United States of America

FIRST EDITION

Acknowledgments

Much of this book was written at Mount Falcon Castle, Ballina, County Mayo, Ireland. The author wishes to express her thanks to the Mount Falcon family, including Dudley, Gay, and Coragh.

In New York, affectionate thanks to Victoria Wilson, Gary Strauss, and the Cornelia Street Café, and friends.

To R and T and B,

with love

Also, for C. W. Aldridge,

with a full and grateful heart

MEDUSA'S GIFT

MAGDALENE

For the record?

I never slept with the president. Therefore all those others who claim to have slept with the one who slept with the president are liars. I never slept with any of them either, of course, but theirs are not the lies that matter to history.

The fact is, however, that had it not been for the first lie, I would not now be, as the Beatles claimed to be in the 1960s, somewhat larger than Jesus, as well as Life. If only because I died a martyr, in my prime, when Hollywood was the sun of God, and a martyr had no need to die a virgin.

The island's light was famous; artists had left home for it, abandoning all other truths. Many had stayed on for years, blinded by its clarity, powerless within it, diluting their daily epiphanies with vermouth cassis, the color of an alarming sunset.

The sun was setting now, as the last afternoon ferry pulled into the perfect curved harbor; rocky hillsides rose from the shore like cupped palms bringing water to a dying friend.

Houses appeared—bright scattered specks, toys lost among the rocks. The one they had rented for Magdalene was set high, facing the sea, a half hour's wearying climb up crumbling paths, scrub, rubble, wild grass. She was not ready. The bags, and the trunks full of her secrets, were left with a donkey driver. She wanted first to walk along the cliffs, while the sea glowed at her feet like a fire. The sea that was not wine dark after all, but ink; authentic navy blue. Tavernas perched above it, tiny strings of lights threading invisibly between them in the trees. Young, tanned bodies dangled precariously over railings; each hand held a stemmed wineglass. Cigarettes moved like wands of amber glow. Shadowed smiles, whispers. American music floated behind them like the strings of lights.

Rob Twist, owner of the American Bar, greeted her warmly, as though they were friends. Glass of wine? Oh, yes! She was breathless with delight, everyone's favorite of her voices. In just . . . a moment, she added suddenly, turning away. Not even waiting for his nod. She strode swiftly to the rocks and dove. He would lean over the dangerous railing with the others, holding deliciously cool wine, admiring her smooth white stroke against the darkness.

She would be alone in the water; apparently no one here swam at this hour. Fools, she thought. How beautiful it is: twilight sea, still warm, rich with the sun's colors. No one who lives daily with beauty ever celebrates it with the pure joy of the astonished stranger. Only once, in America, had she found natives attending their own sunset, cheering and applauding as though it were what it was—a theater of the gods. She dove now open-eyed, discovering rainbows beneath her, icy clarity, silence. Coming up, the first light she saw was the bar owner's smile. She wanted to shout something joyous. She waved instead—phosphorescent foam gleaming along her lifted arm. As she reached upward, raising her head, she felt a soft veil stroke her face; but no, not a veil, a substance—invisible, wetter than the sea itself, a fleeting, solid thing, warm, like streaming flesh, a living creature.

The sensation was gone in an instant, like a caress, igniting her face, electrifying it. Then a searing flash coursed along her body, as though she herself had become charged, a live wire. Thrilling. She screamed. The figures draped over the railing moved, shouted; their cigarette tips swooped and darted now like fireflies in distress.

The bar owner seemed to stand transfixed, holding two wineglasses; she saw his handsome English face shimmer in the haze as she thrashed her blind way toward him, toward the sheltering rocks; her limbs jerking with successive spasms of shock and terror. What was it?

A crowd had gathered: sympathetic, incomprehensible murmurs, gestures. Rob Twist barked an order; someone proffered a vial of clear liquid, accompanied by gestures. Quick! Rub hard, where it struck. Another wave of shock had set her trembling; she could not grasp the bottle. She tried to speak; her tongue swelled against her voice.

Doctor? She heard other voices, shouting now. A babel of alarming sounds. Doctor! She saw Rob Twist, still a blur, scribbling something, a name, address; saw fans of open hands, fingers webbed, pointing upward toward the black hills.

Two strangers grasped her arms to lead her away, when suddenly a young girl plucked at her. Look! The girl commanded, turning her naked back, exposing a mass of flame-colored streaks, lash marks, hideous scarred welts. *Méduse!* hissed the girl, holding up a finger. Ago year! Or die to it.

The drinkers nodded, all still talking at once. No one swims at this hour, said one. In the sun-colored water one cannot see it coming.

Blind! Disfigured! she screamed at the strangers half-carrying her through the black maze of streets. I have come here to die after all.

No! they shouted back. Or *neh,* meaning yes.

Doctor; injection; stream of words like the sound of her name under water; darkness; drugged sleep. If she did not die this night of shock or allergy, to the *méduse* sting or to the medicine, she would at least survive.

Before surrendering to the drug, she pleaded with the doctor, in mime. Blind? Scarred? Face? Tongue?

You have been *medusée,* he said, apologetic. The strangers who had brought her agreed politely. *Neh.* No one here swims at this hour.

At the bar, Rob Twist waits for word. Not of the stung woman, but of the rich guests he has been expecting since the previous summer. The regulars exchange amused glances behind his back. What do you think that woman's story is? murmurs one, a painter with thin shoulders, who no longer paints.

No one answers him, and after a minute he answers himself. No story, he says. That's why she's here. To invent one.

Rob Twist laughs, a pitch higher than he intended. That why you came? Or why you're still here?

The painter sighs. Dear boy, I came because I knew you'd give me a drink. Eventually. Rob refills the proffered glass. Can't roll you up the hill tonight, however. Company's coming.

Let me guess. Poets or spies?

Both, says Rob brightly. I know you prefer when they're both. Actually it's Ran Pollexfen. And his new sultan.

Ah, says the painter, who has not been listening. What about the woman, though? The stung one.

Famous, Rob assures him. Utterly famous. So I'm told. My sources usually lie, though. Why would anyone famous rent the worst house on Sea-Squirt Lane?

Fame don't pay, mutters the painter, staring into his reemptied glass. Or was that crime?

At the other end of the bar, the young girl with the scarred back says, in perfect English, She won't be able to show her face in here for some time. Lucky bitch. Whoever she was.

It happened that this was the summer when misfortune struck in threes—as it so often does. A powerful politician died in the arms of his scandalously young mistress, who vanished before the evening news. Then a reigning sex goddess was reported dead of an accidental overdose—of love, age, neglect, or some other proscribed substance. Finally a falling star tumbled from a chartered yacht sailing in shark-infested waters, leaving a stunned husband and (his or her) lover on board.

On several continents there followed much sifting of contradictory evidence; mournful sighing and shocked whispers, and the awful sound of official silence. Bodies of water were dragged; funeral services held; historical footnotes composed. But the truth of each tragedy receded with every retelling.

So it was that the scarred girl's chance remark, carelessly tossed into the stale air of the American Bar, set Rob Twist thinking. Twist was a man whose thoughts were rarely idle; indeed, with the bar failing and the island itself about to be dropped from the itineraries of two major cruise lines, he could no longer afford the luxury of idleness in any form.

Whenever he thought, furthermore, Rob Twist acted at once. The moment was seized. First, he paid the donkey driver who had been entrusted with the lady's luggage to make a brief stop with it—perhaps an hour—at Rob's own house on Sea-Squirt Lane. It was hardly out of the man's way.

Then he sent several cables to New York, Atlanta, Waco, Texas; to a boat marina in Cyprus, to Kizlar, to the mainland bank that held an interest in the house that Rob himself had managed to rent, sight unseen, to someone utterly famous.

This particular house had never been grand enough for

the discriminating traveler who booked lodgings through the better mainland agents, or through the glossy classified ads in Hide/Away International. But then the island itself was less grand than it had been. The visitors clustered here this season were an odd lot—black-sheepish remittance men of good family; once-promising (never-fulfilling) artists like the thin-shouldered drunk, Tarik Pailthorpe; recovering poet-novelists; Americans who had divorced unprofitably; hastily retiring businessmen with something more serious than money to hide. Rob Twist himself fit most of these categories, which was why he had long ago become so perfectly suited to this place, and to his place in it.

Rob's cables were all identical, and very carefully worded: Reason to believe something of value to you has arrived. When may we expect you?

The first to respond was Terry Mould, whom Rob had deliberately neglected to wire. The call came from London at 4 a.m., island time. Collect. Rob smiled in his sleep. Who've you got, then? the unmistakable voice demanded.

That you, Terry? Thought you were in Kabul.

Mould ignored this. Who've you got? he said again. Is it Magdalene? It is, isn't it?

Rob's laugh was as light as he could make it. Will the missus be coming with you? he asked, pleasantly. Tell herself the plumbing's fixed. And we've bought her a pink bidet.

Terry Mould, England's most illustrious independent filmmaker, made an unintelligible noise, and hung up.

Who was that? murmured Rob's wife, Ione, into her tear-stained pillow.

Everyone, said Rob happily. He might have to get the plumbing repaired at Quinet's house before Mould arrived. He might even have to pay for it out of his own pocket. Call it an investment. Magdalene would pay him back. She would indeed.

By the following afternoon, as the midday heat subsided and the water came back on, the recipients of Rob's cryptic message had been heard from. Rats returning to the sunken ship, raised from the depths, brimming with pirate's treasure, also known as fool's gold.

Grace Craven's reply was the shortest. Oh, I doubt it, was what she wired. Within an hour she had apparently reconsidered. A second dispatch, this signed by her university publishers, informed Mr. Twist that Professor Craven would stop briefly after all, en route to the Ajaccio Film Festival. Rob smiled. Professor Craven always traveled the low road to her exotic destinations. The stop at Medusa would double her fare. It was time to find out whether he had lied to her—to all of them, including himself.

His preliminary search of Magdalene's luggage had yielded an interesting mess. Interesting, Rob would be first to say, as in the Chinese curse: May you live in interesting times. Humpbacked chest filled with letters, photographs, film canisters, reels of tape. Diary bearing the initials of an unhappy socialite who shot her husband. Nude pictures of a serene princess, the body considerably older than she had been when her car plunged over a cliff. Memo composed on the special italic typewriter of a senator, dated the day of his wife's fatal overdose. Paranoid note on ecru vellum notepaper, signed by an heiress who had been in an irreversible coma for a decade.

Rob rummaged through the lot, snapped as many copies as his ancient Praktina would hold, carefully closed the trunk, and sent the driver on to his destination. He had found something, all right. Never mind what.

The strangers waited with Magdalene until it could be safely assumed that she would not die in the doctor's brown waiting room. They escorted her up the dark hill to her home, murmuring assurances. Rob Twist's wife would look in on her tomorrow. Anything she needed now, anything at all? She assured them in return: Nothing.

The lights were on in the little bare house; her luggage neatly piled in the center of the largest room. The strangers left her.

Magdalene knew at once that things had been disturbed, that the culprit had been prying, not thieving. Contents of one piece picked over, nothing taken. Sealed metal footlocker untouched. She had packed well. He, they, would be back.

MAGDALENE

I told him I was pregnant. Told him I would make a mess. His wife already knew. I told him that. He was very drunk, I'm sure he was, but he wanted me then, still, even so, wanted me—or wanted the mess. He liked smashing things up for the family, the only way they ever noticed him anyway. He said, I'll kill you, or I ought to kill you, and I said, I suppose so but it won't help, I've already written it, my lawyer has a copy, and my analyst, one for the press—and you said you loved me, so now you can prove it. I shouldn't have laughed the way I did; he thought I was losing it, thought I might . . . really hurt him that way. Of course I was bluffing, though; he ought to have known, I never would—I mean I knew how he was, still terrified of his family, wanting so badly for everyone to think he deserved to be alive when, well, when the "good" brother wasn't—

But I never meant to grab the wheel, never meant to push him, never thought he'd hold me down—I still can't believe he did that, hold me down after we hit the water—I thought, I swear I thought, he loved me. His baby—I only wanted—

13

The largest house on the island was abnormally lit up, as though something worse than a party were about to happen. The Pollexfens' new friend, the sultan of Kizlar, had come to escape a spell of unpleasant climate in his own country. An ear might have followed him on the last ferry from the mainland. Or possibly not an ear. Maybe a thumb was coming, or a testicle. In any case an urgent message. The sultan was not going to be upset. It was hardly the first body part he had ever received by express courier, while on vacation. Sign here, please.

Ran Pollexfen tried to set a relaxed tone with rare old recordings of the late king of Thailand on tenor sax. "Honeysuckle Rose." "Ain't Misbehavin'." How they loved the American soul in the mysterious East, back then. But the multicolored sultanas of Kizlar remained inscrutable. Whispering thinly veiled insults. Missing their VCRs in the blue-tiled seraglio.

The message arrived as promised. Soggy; blood seeping through the Jiffy bag. The sultan eyed it with distaste. God, he breathed, in Kizlari. Let it not be testicles.

Ran Pollexfen was on the terrace shaking seabreezes in a crystal pitcher. He did not stop shaking as the messenger made his way past him, leaving a trail across the white stone floor, like a splashy bougainvillea. Needs more grenadine, Ran murmured, frowning at the pale froth in the pitcher.

The air in the American Bar was different too. Charged, as if the *méduse* had struck them all. Rob Twist seemed barely under control; his limbs twitched like those of a small-time eccentric dancer, just when the producer comes to catch his act. Two high spots of ruddle stained his English cheeks, fever pink, like sheep markings. And those liquid eyes, one blue, one gold, beseeching the front door. At last it swung open, revealing Pollexfens. Pavilioned in splendor. Just popped in, no time for a drink. Evening-pajamaed, stickpinned, cravatted. So curried and rich-voiced. Mrs. with the quick brown movements of the celebrated fox, nemesis of lazy dog. Gold flashed at her ears, circled her neck, wrists, fingers. Her trousers flowed like silk rivers. Hello, there, she said. "There" pronounced as though it were Rob Twist's name. Sliding smile, double air-kisses. We're expecting . . . half nine, the sultan, you know, very just us.

Rob nodded, too brightly. Brilliant, yes, quite understand, and Ione of course. He would have a case of something donkeyed up, no trouble. They were gone before he could curtsy.

He would have to leave the bar early, supervise his wife's costume. The regular drunks—he counted them—five; he shook his head, clearing it. Bloody hell. Whoever was here at closing time would follow his conscience. Or just lock them all in with the booze and the distempered cats.

He hurried up the path, racing his thoughts. It was true that Magdalene once faked her own death. Well, disappeared. Height of her fame, or just past it. Missing for a month. Having left a trail of false scent. Weren't there notes, tickets, a diary? And then she turned up dazed on somebody's yacht somewhere. Boat called *Star Immaculate*. Good career move, everyone snidely said. "Lost" Magdalene photographs already selling for zillions. Originals of early nudes she'd tried to suppress. All her dreadful films brought back, sold out, creamed over. She went out there an old foozle, came back an icon. . . . *Star Immaculate?* Pollexfen's boat?

Now, had she gone and done it again? No accident, no crime? Or was this faker not even the faker herself?

Well, but those trunks. Self-serving great pack of lies, doubtless. But unlike all other versions, other people's lies. These were lies from the mouth of the world's sweetest horse. Magdalene here; Magdalene his. Why shouldn't she have a piece of the Magdalene pie? Rob Twist could afford to cut her one. Dead Magdalene was earning an indecent living for thousands. Live Magdalene, what are we bid? Rob smiled generously, savoring the thought of Grace Craven, Terry Mould, the Modern, the new film institutes at Texas, Atlanta. All of them on their way. Even now. What are we bid for the president's mistress? the senator's mistake? What will we give for proofs positive of her colored blood, Sapphic tendencies, politically sensitive abortion? Figment of surgery, media wet dream, victim of the century. Or just another aging bimbette, to be laid. To rest. Either way, he concluded happily. The cash flows here. He gazed with a fond, nostalgic sigh at the rubble that passed for his doorstep on Sea-Squirt Lane. Everything plausible, best of all plausible worlds.

Rob found his wife in their bedroom, reading aloud to the children. *Alice in Wonderland.* Their eyes had already glazed over. The younger one wanted *Ariadne auf Naxos.* Andromeda and the sea monster. The older one wanted Queen Omphale in the lion's skin, enslaved Hercules doing women's work. We're going to the Pollexfens' for drinks, Rob announced. Put on something native.

Ione glared at him. Kidding, he said. But he never was, with her. He wanted her in clinging white, displaying generous dollops of succulent golden flesh. She preferred loose printed crepe, dull colored, ankle deep, neck high. He sighed. The sultan's eyes would not light. And if the sultan's eyes did not light, the Pollexfens might not bring him and his checkbook to the bar, And if . . .

Ione, he said, go and put on that white thing—the one —he gestured.

She made a face, but said nothing. Then she closed the book, kissed the girls, brushed past him. He decided not to stay, watching her; better to wait downstairs. Thinking if he didn't press, perhaps she would—bloody hell she would. He poured himself a drink. Strong. Hating her. Goddamning her. The bitch would come down in mourning weeds, to spite him. Just once, just once, couldn't she, but of course she couldn't. Because if Pollexfen ever came through, bar and island saved from drowning, Ione would be marooned. Never to get to England, never to save her daughters from their accursed Greekness.

He poured himself another Metaxa. One more. Needed ten minutes anyway. Needed to reread something Grace

Craven had written about Magdalene, just after the accident. Some highbrow film quarterly had killed it. Scurrilous libel. Rob had to do some favors to get a copy. He had figured that any scurrilous libel by Grace Craven would be worth owning. It was in a folder marked "?".

Lovers knot; the triangle; mysterious watery grave. Magdalene reclaimed by the sea, like Venus, pulled down by her ropes of hair, and pearls, and radiance. She died after a night of rich quarrels. At the far edge of her beauty, full-blown, her skin silken, like roses on the last good day.

But in her eyes, fear was already visible. In her last films she wore the startled look of a pampered child whose parents have lost everything, or have abandoned her.

In fact she *was* a child abandoned, having outlived our belief in her innocence. The night she vanished, her two men had not even wanted her with them. Until then, they had been together, the three, the couple and their inseparable friend, that handsome devil. A classic triangle. Only Father, Son, and Holy Spirit surpasses it.

The world smiles at the romance it calls *ménage à trois*. The world thinks it understands. The woman thinks she does too.

Magdalene, however, was, by profession, nobody's fool. She had been a beauty too many years. Men drawn to beauty such as hers are often secretly drawn to each other; they gaze together, each imagining himself in her, her in himself. And in this gazing, this imagining, each discovers the other. The true beauty they fall to loving is their own. She becomes the pretext. If they quarrel, the world always knew they would quarrel over her. Whereas the trouble may be distinctly of another order—how to abandon her, how to dissolve the union, sustain the performance, satisfy the romance of the romance. Lancelot and Arthur? Antony and Caesar? JFK and RFK?

The night Magdalene fell or dived or jumped overboard, during the notorious moonlight picnic cruise, she had, by all accounts, consumed more wine than either of her men was accustomed to seeing her drink. Indeed, they both recalled later that they had exchanged glances of concern, watching her. Upset about something. She had been counting on a thing that now wasn't going to happen, unless one of them made it happen, which they could hardly afford just now. A part she said she'd kill for. Buy rights to some book and then do a deal no one wanted, the usual.

Magdalene was not such a name or face to be reckoned with, anymore, was the trouble. And she refused to just go away, just disappear out of their faces. Palms would need to be greased, palms that never needed lubrication before. Her agent was busy, had money calling on another line.

They had secured the house for her, gates, alarms, dogs, guards. Since the rumors about Magdalene and the president, and nobody was complaining, mind you, it had done none of them any harm, but since the rumors, there had been mail, and telephone threats, strange cars idling nearby, of course it was disturbing. She was, suddenly, a politically sensitive issue, and even if none of it was her fault, which it wasn't, they *knew* that, of course they did, but even so, it was a trying time.

They had both been seeing a lot of their friend, the actor William Hack. Will was a brick; thank God he was in their lives just then, one hated to think what it would have been like if Will hadn't been around. Matter of fact, they had talked him out of a project that would have taken him away for six months. Hey, pal, if you can possibly say no or later, even just later, I sure, Magdalene and I, I mean, would sure feel better having you around just now, you know, you're the only one who can make her laugh when she's hysterical, which (and here eyes would have rolled, wickedly, helplessly, heavenward, man-to-manly) God knows she is these days, pre-menopausal, pre-menstrual, pre-suicidal, pre-over-the-hill, pre-pain-in-the-ass, whatever, no telling, probably all of the above, eh? And the two of them would have punched each other hard, for emphasis, and that would somehow release them to laugh, or get a couple more beers, couple more lines, or clap each other on the back, embrace, get more beers, like that.

Which was how it must have been that night, near as they could remember, whatthehell, she, Magdalene, had been right there with them until suddenly she wasn't, who the hell knew, maybe she had the rag on, or was sleepy like they get, you know, all that wine, and the—whatever was eating her, the part she didn't get, their not coming through with a sworn affidavit that they would buy her the goddamn rights to the book, or the play, or whatever it was, or maybe it was that the president himself wouldn't buy it for her, or build her a goddamn Washington monument, who the hell knew, what occasion he hadn't, so to speak, risen to, it wasn't that though, they could both swear to that, it was the *last* thing the lady wanted, believe it, she was in no mood for that, believe it. Uh-huh, the detectives said, not looking at them, either of them, just writing it down. So that's, ah, *that,* then, unless, they said, letting it trail off in a non-threatening way. Mmm, uh, ah. Embarrassed is what everyone was; sympathetic too.

Women who jumped or fell were, let's face it, something you hadda sympathize with a guy, especially a famous guy, and especially, you know, woman that age, not too steady on her pins like they get, *you* know. So, then, the boats went out and dragged the area, and nothing came up, and after three four days they quit, and said it'll wash up someplace sometime and we haven't got the equipment, the manpower, you understand it's not we don't think it's important, but.

And that was it, which is maybe more casual than in the States, but on the Continent it was considered exhaustive, historically unprecedented, last time they ever had so many fishing boats out was W.W. II, believe it.

So, not a trace. The story moves inexorably from prime-time news to the marginal press, supermarket tabloids, where relics of the true body may yet wash ashore at Valletta or Mitilini. Suicide notes will be found, bombshell diaries, secret love letters from world leaders and dead rock stars, a mob lawyer's Magdalene file, an abortion clinic's records, with an appointment for "Belle Salop," scheduled three days after she disappeared.

It was almost an anticlimax when the husband died two weeks later in the wreck of his friend's antique sports car, during the Glasgow–Monaco race. Poor guy was not in racing form.

Officials have declined further comment. We await now the memoir of the boat's captain, the shocking confessions of Magdalene's maid, former secretary, therapist.

Her house has been sold. Contractors say the bills for that new alarm system, and the gates, were never paid. Will Hack recently set off for a cruise of islands off the Turkish coast. I want to see where the Virgin was assumed to Heaven, he said. Tears in his eyes.

It was curious that, after the accident, Hack never appeared on deck while the news cameras were there. A spokesman said he was in shock. Having not made a film in over two years, he may have suffered a premonition that this would not be good for his career.

William Hack: somehow the world is uncomfortable now about William Hack. If he was Magdalene's last lover, the world disapproves. After the president? And what if, as is increasingly rumored, the story is something else, something really unsavory. If the men were the lovers, say, and Magdalene had discovered it. One safely assumes the world has no stomach for that. Hack's face looks odd to us now, shifty, something reptilian about it. Something of a killer. Although that would be, in itself, O.K.; killers have a certain macho charm, if they're straight. That is, if they rape and kill in fits of lust or jealous rage. Like a man. But not if they're . . . funny that way.

Rob heard Ione's step behind him. He would not look up. Ready, she said. Icy. Hating him.

She was encased in a black robe, shapeless as an Anglican bishop.

No, he said, under his breath.

No?

They stood facing each other, perhaps three feet apart, leaning like boxers. Then he turned his back to her.

Oh, Rob, she said, softly.

He said nothing, nor did he move.

Damn you! she screamed then, whirling backward, her thick chimere spiraling after her like a storm.

He replaced the folder and went on sipping his drink until she reappeared, white gowned, meek as a sacrifice. Her face said that he would pay for the victory. He slapped her for the threat. A single stinging backhanded slap, sudden and swift, forcing her backward, summoning tears. She whispered something, some Greek curse.

The Pollexfens had never before issued an invitation to Rob Twist. It was as close to a royal summons as could be achieved in a colony of outcasts. Without it one could spend a summer or a lifetime wandering these hot, empty streets, gazing at the dead, white eyes of cool stone houses. Even the gardens bloomed secretly behind walls, never exposing themselves to strangers. One might own a bar here or merely drink oneself to death. One was free to dive, at one's risk, into the sea; to dabble in exotic drugs or real estate; to buy worthless trinkets in the harbor shops. But no bright-painted door would open, nor the heart behind a single smiling face. A passerby, a tourist, a bar owner is someone whom one need never consent to know. Islands, such as Medusa, noted for the friendly wave, signifying Hello, There.

Long ago and in another country, Ran Pollexfen had made his fame and squandered his fortune playing on those teams of laughing playboys often used in pairs to bracket a spangled lady on a zebra banquette. Inevitably, one of the spangled centerpieces was Magdalene. The rumor that he-and-she . . . had transformed him forever in the world's twinkling eye, from one of a set to one of a kind.

Inevitably, too, Magdalene slipped into subtler gowns, escorts, banquettes. Pollexfen and his yacht, bearing her lipstick's traces, set sail for lesser islands, lesser lights.

Half a life and world away, he had found Myrrha, his ebony goddess. Ran thought, or Myrrha claimed, that she was the wayward child of a fanatical Senoussi chieftain; besotted by such wildness, Ran chased her from one Seychelle to another (Seychelles, Seychelles by the seyshore, as he put it), only to find that she was a Canadian law-school dropout, with terrorist leanings. She was also pregnant. Raped, she said, by an emerging strongman.

Predictably, Pollexfen married her anyway. They had three colorful babies. His family disinherited him. But between his old friends and her old enemies, they had remade his fortune several times over. What with helpful errands for troubled bankers and political leaders. Spectacularly discreet cruises with a sealed cargo of the over-famous, the illegal, and the filthier rich.

While Ran thus pursued (and pandered to) other people's happiness, Myrrha settled into island life, marred only by occasional unpleasantness—assassination and blackmail attempts; the defection, at fifteen, of her potentially embarrassing firstborn son.

Ran had lately installed a grotto here in their enormous basement—the only private pool on the island—so that Myrrha, their guests, and the remaining children could swim safe from ill-wishers, stinging sea creatures, and public stares.

The night of the sultan, the night of Magdalene, several dozen guests were crowded about the subterranean poolside, sipping drinks of improbable colors, beakers of neon light. The red ones were Bloody Myrrhas, potent concoctions centering on the biblical fruit of Pollexfen's glass-walled mini-Eden. The sulphurous yellow was Citron, made from the pungent local lemon, large as grapefruit, whose perfume had inspired English poets and caused historic shipwrecks.

Myrrha herself was swathed in a vermilion pareo; rings of ivory coiling about her bared limbs. Cobra Woman,

Rob thought, lacking only the serpent throne and chorus of enchanted rattlers. Unless her guests would do.

He gulped one of the Bloody Myrrhas, pronounced it delicious, and found himself instantly drunk. The brown children in the glowing green pool, riding plastic dinosaurs, took on an eerie fairy-tale aspect. Every sound in the tiled cavern seemed to shimmer and echo before one heard the words themselves, or understood that the laughter might be a response to something said a moment ago, or a moment hence. He blurted things carelessly. Amusing stories about a star, a sting, and a stream of important visitors, summoned by Rob Twist, even now, on their way. No one appeared to be listening.

Myrrha Pollexfen admired Ione Twist's cheap plastic sandals. Perhaps she was insincere, but Rob insisted she take them; he would buy his wife another pair. In return Myrrha confided her latest dream, establishing an orphicist wellness center on the island. She had, she said, studied organotherapy with a master in Sri Lanka. Ran, she said, was being most supportive. Their marriage having already weathered the storms of her meetings with Corsican nationalists, and the eldest boy's bolting to join a pack of itinerant beach rats. Ran Junior (for so they had named him), had become one of the mostly naked young who wove grass huts and lived in clusters, on vacant stretches of sand, at the far ends of the larger islands. They wore shredded denim when they rode the buses to buy tinned food in the villages, or when they grew restless, or got money from home to push on to some other island. Many had been living the life for ten years or more; some now had babies strapped or slung upon their bellies or backs.

By now they were a wild race, beyond language or the reach of ordinary social rule. They seemed to need very little; they had learned to weave the grass tightly enough to keep themselves dry; they ate the tinned food and the occasional fish.

They looked fit enough, wiry but strong, the color of their eyes as bleached out as their hair, as the sandy wastes themselves.

Some of them had guitars; some of them sang. There were always many miles between their encampments and the civilized villages. The police never bothered them, and few tourists trekked far enough out to discover them. If any did, they made no sign of noticing.

Ran and Myrrha had not heard from the boy in two years; his last card bore a Turkish postmark, but any friend might have carried it for months, in a jeans pocket, a rucksack, from Agadir or Tunis, until it tumbled out one day in Kushadesi, with a crumple of cigarettes and bus stubs, and someone slid it into a postbox. He wrote that he had a child, a son. But his girlfriend took it; he thought they might have gone to Kizlar. Wasn't that where some sultan had force-fed his concubines on morsels of their own breasts?

Regretfully, the present sultan of Kizlar was to inform his hosts after the guests had gone, the package he had received earlier contained what appeared to be a child's mangled thumb or penis, wearing a ring that Myrrha Pollexfen knew well. It had once caused her to bleed internally. Her lover, the developing despot, had later had her name cut into it. His primitive way of evening the score. She didn't remember telling him about the baby.

Rob reached home well before his wife, who now had to negotiate the stony path barefoot, in the dark. For your sins, Rob called to her, over his shoulder, as he ran. He needed to shut himself in with his anglepoise lamp, magnifying glass, and the handful of purloined paper that had better change his life.

MAGDALENE

I was the one who insisted Willie come with us—that was the biggest joke. Bobby actually argued with me—Will would spoil it. He'd bring this great hash. He'd want to play charades: Moon over Miami. He'd get up on the bar and tap-dance—strip off his clothes, drink himself nasty—and we'd all have to hold his head. But *I* said Will needs to come with us, we can't leave him, he'll be miserable. And we owe him, I owe him, that time in New York he found you crazed in that woman's loft, and carried you home—God, I could have lost you that night, don't you know that, I owe him, you owe him. So Bobby came up behind me and kissed me, for being so—what—noble? generous? humane? But it was this huge fucking joke, all the whole time. It was—they were—I was the *beard,* dig it? Little Ms. movie star, Ms. screen queen. My sexiest role—the girl in the sandwich. Who'da thunk it? Who'd believe it? And anyway who'd care? The answer is nobody, *personne, nadie, ningún*—forget it. I mean the woman's a nutcase, just make the little magic gesture, index finger tapping the temple. They'll come and take her away—I mean if she *should* happen to surface, which is doubtful. We did, after all, dope her a little. Had to. She walked in. You know how they get, they see something, think they see something. Will would have shrugged. Bobby at least would have been embarrassed. But Will—can't you see him, so cool, stoned, poker-faced—Will would have shrugged. She must have gone in for a swim.

But she never swam. They said. Never used her own pool. And it was midnight. No moon.

He shrugged again. Annoyed now. Man, what do I know. So she hated pools. Even Esther Williams preferred oceans. Mermaids shouldn't drink and dive. Let alone do dope. But she *said* she was going . . . in . . . for a swim. His eyes were so white—empty, like corpse eyes. Bobby never said a word. I know. Of course I know. Doesn't matter what really happened. What matters is what they thought.

Buried my wife at sea, Bobby sobbed on the TV news. They filmed the ceremony—tossing white roses overboard. Bobby could look serious with cameras on him. Grave, he looked—watery grave. Poor kid, he blubbered; then his voice broke. Just a little throat catch, really. But that *was* the catch. Everyone knew the punch line: He was leaving me for Willie Hack. And all the time I thought *I* was leaving *him* for Willie Hack. Wouldn't that *jar* you?

I made a scene, it's true, they were pissed. And I threatened a press conference. Will panicked. Bobby said, Don't—she wouldn't—I swear she wouldn't. But Will couldn't calm down. His contract. His best-supporting nomination. He came at me with the broken Veuve Clicquot bottle. Bobby tried—I guess he tried—to get in the way. Doesn't matter. I screamed, backed against the rail, and when—when he lunged at me, with that bottle aimed at my face, I twisted away—slipped, lost my balance—or he touched me, and the rail gave way, and I went . . . over. They could have—yelled, Stop—or run to the crew and made them circle back. I guess they stared at each other for a minute, neither of them moving, or saying anything. And then the minute passed. The boat slipped on, slicing the black water. You know? The minute, and the panic, and the problem, gone. After that they couldn't see much, no moon, and even if I was still screaming you couldn't hear it—that's the thing about moving fast in the water. Anything that might upset you is gone, just like that. Silent, black, gone. Like a movie. The end—

Rob switched off his lamp and sat in the dark, waiting for the Bloody Myrrhas to wear off. Pollexfen's boat? he mused. Did Grace Craven know? What else did Grace Craven know? And who killed the story? He fell asleep, in the chair, musing.

Grace Craven was the one who sprang to mind with the phrase "too smart for her own good." She was at the age —hovering over forty, awaiting landing instructions— when women were expected to see that they had got everything that was coming to them. Only a few greedy graspers remained milling about, counting their short change. Believing still that men found them cute when angry.

Grace would never make that particular mistake. Even at close range she never seemed ambitious. She performed her spectacular career like a Miss America finalist, fingering her Chopin prelude faultlessly, with a slightly puzzled smile, as though she wondered where that lovely music could be coming from.

She had her singular child, a daughter; her second no-fault divorce; her distinguished, if untenured, professorship; her desirable, if married, gentleman caller; and a dozen quite serviceable old friends.

A serious person, you would say; a success. Not so enviable as to force you to push her into a wet snowdrift, or to steal an arcane movie memento from her preposterous collection. Ouspenskaya's cane. Sonja Henie's skate laces. Disney's rejection memo for a Snow White with breasts.

Still, one could scarcely imagine how often Dr. Grace Craven revised and updated her secret list of important things that were missing. Not from her collection. Not from her life, either. Marriage, for instance, was definitely not on her current agenda, a fact that set her apart from her women friends, and made them trust her both more and less. More, because at their holiday parties she did not stand, squinty-eyed and gussied up, at the edges of their rooms, mentally sorting the couples whose husbands might be ripe for uncoupling. Less, because she might—must—be devious.

Well, she was headstrong. Hepburn might have played her once, or Magdalene herself. The sort of woman who, when all about her were fleeing into remarriages with men who suffered terribly from alcohol and hair loss, would suddenly decide to chuck everything and go chase a rainbow, or a wild goose. Or shades of Magdalene.

Magdalene was perhaps Grace Craven's most endearing weakness. Early Magdalene, actually. The films in which the heroine wore silver gowns curved almost insupportably low in back to reveal her magnificent shoulders. In those films, Grace had observed, shoulders were breasts. She had written eloquently of the obligatory ocean-crossing scene, in which Magdalene always stood, gleaming naked back to camera, against a white railing, gazing out at a moonlit sea, her silent lover beside her, a death figure in his black dinner clothes. Smoke from their cigarettes curling suggestively as tango dancers, then drifting into the darkness of their separate destinies.

It was even predictable that Grace should choose precisely the wrong moment to pursue this chimera of hers. Magdalene projects dying by the score, despite the unslakable public thirst for posthumous scandal. Ghostly afterimages continued to fill newspapers and television screens. Magdalene as a slightly cross-eyed child; Magdalene kissing the president; the famous backward-upside-down pose, with her head between her legs; and the one in the Rome hospital, with the Pope, after her near-death from, supposedly, flaking Sistine Chapel paint. It was becoming clear that while some forms of Magdalene would sell forever, others were as dead in the water as she was.

Neither Grace's publishers, nor her academic mentors, were easily persuaded, even by Grace, that she should set aside her long-awaited study of adultery in postwar film noir. From a serious film-historic view, Magdalene was a minor figure, one who would be dead a very long time. Whereas the theme of adultery . . . the publisher, willing to commit, without a line written.

It was S. Z. Hroch, finally—or Hroch's intense, though unannounced, interest in acquiring Magdalene for the Museum of the Arts' hugely endowed new film-history wing—that prompted Grace's sudden leap. In fact it was something Hroch had said long ago, when they had first become lovers, something about what Magdalene might someday be worth to the museum. Or to the new film archive at Texas. Or to the Atlanta Institute. That is, of course, if there turned out to be stuff of any real significance. Anything pertaining to the president. Or the senator. Or even a single note from—

Grace had once heard S. Z. Hroch lecture on the textures of a Magdalene movie—literally, just the textures: skin, satin, lacquer, fur. Expanse of white breast, innocent of cleavage. Glittering diamanté straps, cutting provocatively into the soft whiteness. White fur sleeves. Fur capelets, tippets, gauntlets, cuffs, muffs . . . In another life, Grace mused irreverently, the man was a furrier. He would stop the film to say, Look at this—the way that fox stole descends that shoulder. Now watch the pulse in her throat. We need no other dialog. The fox, and the throat. Telling us she is aroused, but she will resist. Wearily. It seems as great an effort either way. Only Magdalene could convey torpor as steam.

The film was *Faithless*. By then Magdalene had perfected the character—almost-fallen, near-hussy, nice girl who finishes lost. The story was the same as always: will-she-won't-she, God help her if she does. Hroch called Magdalene a Greek-mythic rape victim. The wife who never falters until Zeus appears brilliantly disguised as her lost husband. In the early Magdalenes, he said, adultery was still a dance. By the last one, it was only a deal—a bad deal.

Grace nodded at that; not bad. But look! Hroch was saying. The other man here is a dick. A private dick!

Grace suppressed a shake of her disapproving head. She permitted herself an inaudible sigh. Hroch went on: . . . hired by her rich impotent husband to sail off with Magdalene, seduce her. One kiss. One . . . *kiss*. She yields, she's done for—scarlet, broke, ruined. The dick's expense account is unlimited. Magdalene's is, as always, limited. One . . . kiss.

S. Z. Hroch's audience was deeply moved. Brilliant, said Grace Craven carefully. And repeated it in print, even as she toyed with his fur fetish, in her memorable piece about Magdalene's worst failure, *Train Bleu*. The one where she kissed a stranger good-bye in an empty Paris railway carriage. Grace Craven noted how the dialog, written by an avowed gay male scenarist, had given the film its peculiar chastity. The entire business, eighty-three minutes, involves a single closed-mouth kiss in a parked coach. Not even a Pullman. The couple get arrested, charged with a criminal offense. Magdalene goes into a suicidal panic: she's just a nice bored wife far from home. And the fellow, played by Will Hack, is just as nice. It's Paris; can he help it if a lady tourist wants to see his Eiffel Tower?

Of course, Grace wrote, "The film should have been a homosexual *Brief Encounter.* Because no way would *that* couple be arrested for *that* kiss in *that* station. Never mind what the director was doing—he was in another movie entirely. Strange colors and shadows, deaf-mute urchins, menacing old men dropping oranges, nuns, fainting *enceintes,* leering soldiers . . .

"And poor Magdalene. In her smart two-piece suit with mink tippet. Only once does she take off the fur: in the train car, when they are . . . together. She slides it down her tweed shoulder, and zap! the flics are there, with the flashlights. Twenty years after *Faithless* and *I Confess,* Magdalene is still being ruined by mistake. Proving, lest we forget, the Magdalene moral: A girl can't be too careful. Or a fool and her fur are soon parted. Or as S. Z. Hroch has so eloquently said, Just one . . . kiss."

The day S. Z. Hroch escorted Grace Craven through the great collections, both of them wearing the required white cotton gloves, he had insisted on revealing the contents of old Abraham Homolka's million-dollar drawers. She made a crude joke at that; he threw her a solemn warning look, for the benefit of Ms. Dorothea Pfister, curator of the Homolka archive. Hroch then asked Ms. Pfister to leave them, after opening the climate-controlled vault. Books, photographs, manuscripts, spectacles, pens . . . and a series of small sealed metal containers, shaped like bullets. Grace raised a questioning eyebrow. Hroch cleared his throat. It's very common, you know. Film geniuses no less than men of science or letters. Presidents—Grace Craven threw back her head and laughed. You mean—

Of course, said the eminent director in a low voice.

But why?

Because they are the seminal thinkers of their time. Because they assume—

My God, Grace's voice was now a whisper of shock. You are, all of you, mad. Keeping *ejaculate* in a sealed vault, to be examined by scholars? Does one—can one—*touch* it? Does one apply for permission? Is there a form to fill?

Hroch's face drained of color. My dear lady—

I don't mean that *I* would. I just wondered if, say, some other distinguished research fellow ever opened a vial? In the interests of—

The color had returned. Hroch smiled. They're sealed. It is of scholarly interest only to note that some great men consider it of importance to leave—to include—in their bequests—

Grace Craven held a vial between her fingers, turning it with a slow gesture that caused Hroch to perspire.

Do you ever worry that some unscrupulous young woman scholar might—make—unauthorized use of this—ah, material?

Hroch's smile was strained.

Grace prattled on: . . . pregnancy, sue the great man's estate, the museum, claim a share of posthumous royalties—such astonishing possibilities: scandalous—she glanced at him. Oh, my dear sir, I distress you with my foolishness. Forgive me!

Hroch retrieved the vial from her hand, and put it back in its upholstered niche. His gloved fingers were trembling.

How long do you imagine sperms remain viable?

He stared at her as though she had uttered a blasphemy. Perhaps she had.

Shall we? he said, reaching upward to put out the light. Ms. Pfister will want to set things to rights after us.

Of course. Grace Craven slid her white-gloved hand through the director's arm. *Such* a treat, she said.

Do you imagine they—you—might put Magdalene down here next to . . . him?

I have no idea, he replied. Cautious, noncommittal. It would depend, of course.

Not worthy? Contaminating?

Surely not. The voice like liquid. *He* should be delighted with such a charming companion.

But the trustees. She nodded. No question mark at the end.

Well. He guided her smoothly through the silent offices, the cages and catacombs. The important thing, he was saying charmingly, is to have the Magdalene here. And to have *you* here. He patted the hand that rested on his dark expensive sleeve. *Such* a delight.

But the trustees, she said again.

Not to worry. He smiled, in the way a man smiles when his new teeth do not quite fit. Checking them discreetly with his tongue. Moving his lips as though he were a ventriloquist prompting an invisible dummy. Suddenly he turned toward her. How I wish we had known each other years ago. I feel as though we had; do *you?* Have you been to Kizlar? I'm meant to go next summer, you know. Would you consider it? We could have *such* a time. Indeed we could. Grace Craven smiled her smile in return. We must talk about the possibility. We must plot. But meanwhile I know I must let you go—

Dear lady. Hroch raised her hand to his lips. He scarcely noticed that it still wore the white cotton gloves issued by Ms. Pfister.

Dear sir, she murmured. I will hear from you then? When the trustees have met? You won't forget?

How. His eyes seemed moist with emotion. Could I.

In the taxi Grace Craven replayed the afternoon. He found her attractive? Her powers had not failed her?

No. S. Z. Hroch was the sort of ugly man who did well with women—especially hungry women; women betrayed by love; older women. Never occurs to such men what it takes for a lady to *get* older. Must be some trick of the natural order that women survive. Not too well, mostly. Not too wisely either. It's a wise old con man who takes that as a given. What was it he said to me? "Have you been to Kizlar? We could have *such* a time."

Oh, I can just see him with the widow Homolka. "How is it you never went on with your own work—how dare you not? These photographs—extraordinary! And your passion for the underbellies of mushrooms! Is there another woman who so understands sensuality? If only I could have seen your eyes on the day you discovered it. What would have become of either of us? But your children would not have been born. And this great house, this garden, your splendid life with Homolka. California! You'd have hated my uprooting you, spiriting you off to

Xauen or the Planar, just when your son needed braces, your youngest daughter's pony refused to jump. And now, here we are, in the midst of your terrifying life—"

"—terrifying?" (Old Mrs. Homolka's eyes are dancing.)

"—so *accounted* for. All its lovely interlocking parts." He would have touched her hand about now, the quarter-inch of delicate skin between pinkie and ring finger. It's an electrifying spot. Because the diamond leans heavily into it? His touch light, lighter than the diamond's. She stiffening, but not moving. Their breathing perfectly matched; he inhaling when she exhales. She noticing this, not certain whether it's an accident. Of course it's not. Nothing Hroch does is an accident. He is a fat, sweaty, ambitious Hungarian. How does one imagine he rose to become director of a great museum? I can see poor Mrs. H., glancing at him, in the heavy-lidded, sidelong way older women think is flirtatious. What's the mandatory retirement age for flirting? Oh, he is a con. I knew it at once, before he touched me with his white glove. He needs to be protected from what I know. If I'm careless, he won't play. The trustees trust him? What if they don't? Even I've heard the rumor—Hroch's all the way down. Someone less fat, sweaty, Hungarian, breathing down his neck; some nice Wasp boy wonder with a Princeton doctorate and a rich wife, richer wife than Hroch's.

My dear lady—

Mrs. Homolka rouses herself with difficulty. I've quite forgotten (she sighs) what it was we were supposed to discuss.

Decide, he amends, gently. We were supposed to decide, dear lady. We've already discussed it. You recall.

The year before he would never have permitted that note—half-note—of impatience. The year before there was no nice Wasp boy with a wife richer than Hroch's.

Actually I *don't* recall, she probably said. Wicked witch. Wrinkling her lifted brow. Or vice versa, in this case. But I know you'll recall for me. I seem to have such trouble recalling, these days. He's forced to chuckle at that, dismiss it, raise his glass to her, have another, whatever it is she insisted on his having (he doesn't drink, can't afford to). He says good night when she says she's tired. Not before. Next day the call comes from his trustees; same time as it's come every day for a week. And he has to say, yet again, that nothing has happened. Old Mrs. Homolka hasn't taken the poison mushroom. He hasn't got what they sent him to get; is he, perhaps, losing his famous touch? He sweats; he can hear them shaking their heads. Goddamn the old—if he didn't know better, he'd swear she was playing him.

Of course he got the Homolka. He'll get the Magdalene too. Not without me, he won't.

He was a boor, a peasant, sweaty and ill-favored. A parvenu. Merely doing his job. Not fooling me, though. A million two for the Magdalene? Without a single vial of sperm?

The taxi sped through wet streets, blurring yellow puddles of light. Million two, she said aloud. Thought you said eight eighty, the driver shouted. Million two, she repeated.

He turned, Yoram Golan did, and fixed her with the

hostile, uncomprehending stare of the desperate, exhausted stranger. That's all right, she said softly. Keep the change.

Grace Craven reminded S. Z. Hroch that they had met before. He remembered. But he frowned, pretending to be not quite certain of the details. Had they shared a taxi? Was it in the rain, after one of his little talks? Yes, yes; she laden with a disreputable briefcase, he with an uncharacteristic tied tongue. He recalled noticing that the boots she wore that day were silly, which made him assume that, research fellow or no, she was silly too. Anserine, he said. Floppy cloth boots, weren't they? Bound up with bright laces. Like the footwear of the homeless. He said. Grace Craven's face was burning; not silly. From that moment she seemed to need to prove it; to force his acknowledgment of it. *Dr.* Craven. Profoundly not silly. To her boots.

"From Venice, the train to Dubrovnik," she jotted one day in a note, left on Hroch's desk. "One might stop at Trieste. Or not."

He was stunned—had she taken the journey; was she suggesting it? Had she only imagined it? Read it in the file of some star whose life she coveted? Magdalene? Undoubtedly. It scarcely mattered. He bought her coffee in the dingy staff cafeteria; they talked of trains and boats. She bought him lunch at a salad bar near the museum; they talked of him, the museum; of her, of Magdalene, of life.

All the notions that struck Grace Craven began to seem magical to S. Z. Hroch. Once she spoke of casting lead into the fire, to read the future in the melt. Hroch did not ask how, why; it only seemed urgent that one do it, that doing it would be at once useful and wonderful. He could imagine the circle of children's faces, ruddy with firelight, shining with trust. She would tell their fortunes in her wonderful voice, her voice that Hroch already carried about in his head, playing its music, its sweet rise and fall, light as sighing, as laughter. Already he needed to hear it, imagined hearing it as he drifted in and out of sleep. What was she saying? From Venice, the train to Dubrovnik.

S. Z. Hroch, to his amazement, wanted to be on that train at once, in Grace Craven's company. She leaning forward, gesturing, gazing out at the blurred green landscape, her profile turned toward him. I'm *starved,* she would suddenly exclaim. Aren't you? Rocky? She called him Rocky! Her appetite was constant and whimsical as a child's; her eyes would widen; she coveted every tray of food that passed on its way to another table. Oh, what is *that?* Could we just have one of those, too—just to taste? Do you mind? Don't you want to? Of course he didn't mind. Of course he wanted to. How could he, how could he not? A taste of everything; everything in its taste.

In her company, Hroch would find his finger straying into the whipped cream, his tongue darting out, licking traces of sweetness from the backs of spoons. She laughed, that pure child's laugh of delight, astonished at the greedy child he had become too—or that she had invented, like an imaginary playmate, for company. S. Z. Hroch, that austere legend, who normally subsisted on fruit, skipped lunch, forgot dinner. Such an ascetic he was, borderline monk. His severity, cultivated over fifty years to impress the likes of Grace Craven, concealed the whipped-cream thief, the little Hungarian refugee. In a stroke, she had uncovered the fool he despised. Why she did it, why she delighted in doing it, he cared not. Daringly, he drank too much in her presence, hoping to expose more of what he had spent his life denying. Together they polished off a bottle of Bull's Blood; then two bottles. S. Z. Hroch who, when in doubt, sipped bubble-free water, no lime.

What was going on? She laughed again, touching his glass with hers. Rocky, she sighed. She approved wholeheartedly. He poured, steady-handed. He was a goner.

How long was it before he understood the seductiveness of her approval? Dare he be his worst self, commit his worst sins? he wondered. Worse yet? Was that truly what she wanted—loved? Certain kinds of worst, at least: Gluttony. Sloth. Lust. She would call them appetites, and praise them. And share them. The authority—one in whom authority is vested—judges what is good. Not *bad,* she will say, admiringly. One was transformed. One grew reckless. Leaving a fashionable restaurant, S. Z. Hroch suddenly swept a half-full jeroboam of Calvados from the bar, enfolding it in his woolen muffler. Grace Craven laughed; she gasped. She adored Calvados. Adored thievery.

They spent a weekend at a country inn. Shopping, Hroch stole a white antique silk scarf, worth hundreds. He hesitated; should he tell her? Would she balk at this? Would she find it not a joke? She discovered the scarf soon after, in their luggage. He confessed he had stolen it for her. She seemed impressed, but, perhaps, did he imagine?

disappointed. He suspected she would have preferred his stealing another scarf, the blue one she had refused to let him buy for her. Still, she had two now. And S. Z. Hroch was suddenly aware that he had stolen the white one for himself.

Wine in the afternoon had been the turning point; or perhaps the decision to have wine came first. If it was a decision. At the time it seemed only an impulse, a celebratory punctuation mark, like the joyful exclamation point at the end of a show title: *Hello, Dolly!*

So that facing each other across a table became a sudden occasion, unlike the coffee break, the salad-bar lunch, or the growing habit of looking forward to the glimpse of a face, absorbed in work, in a booklined carrel five floors away.

That is how romance always begins: not with decision, not even with unspoken assent, but with a subtle alteration of mood, an invisible lifting. As in flying a small plane, the instant when you receive, in the exact center of the body, a physical release. You have lost touch with the ground; you are rising gently from it; you are light. Danger, exhilaration, loosening, loss. Some inward part leaps, and is airborne.

They drank enough to feel it. Knowing there was no aerial chart, no itinerary. Only the lifting.

S. Z. Hroch watched the movements of Grace Craven's mouth as she smiled, laughed; as she spoke and savored the wine. It seemed to him that he was watching a dancer.

The first time he took her home, he knew exactly how it would go. It was as if he had written it. He was in a fever to touch her, to have her trembling, the way women do at the instant fear and desire become one emotion. He wanted certain items of her clothing pulled just to there, disarranged, exposing, framing her. He wanted her to be wearing a belt, pulled tight against her naked waist. A conceit. He had never made love to a research fellow wearing a belt. He wanted to take her on the dark carpet, before the narrow mirror, his wife's mirror, watching his body rise above hers, watching her face change, watching her mouth grow soft, turning lavender, the color of bruises.

She offered no resistance beyond the trembling, beyond the murmur that was of pleasure, or surprise, or assent. At the moment, in the moment, he didn't really care what she meant, what she thought; it was startling not to care; exhilarating. One of the two must always be astonished that the other permits, the other assents, the other, whose name is pronounced in a tone of awe, soundlessly, held on the tongue within the mind, rung like a secret bell.

And it amazed him when it all happened just as he had imagined, that she should seem as delighted by it as he was. What a stroke of extraordinary fortune, he thought, gold in the street, a trick, something must be wrong, must be about to go wrong. She is mocking me in her secret heart, he thought. And then: It doesn't matter. Even more amazing.

You, she was saying. You. He realized that she was smiling; he searched the corners of the smile for traces of mockery, for the trick, denial, recantation.

Did you know that you wanted this? she said. When, how did you know?

Hroch shook his head, lying. Better than explaining. They dressed in silence; they went out and walked along the river, then found a restaurant that would serve a blood-rare steak at four in the afternoon. They passed a well-dressed man who had fished a crumpled newspaper out of a trashcan and was reading, intently, even as the deposited waste of someone's dog rolled out of the news and plopped back into the trashcan.

They stood watching the man; still reading, unperturbed. Then they collapsed into successive waves of wild laughter, staggering against the sides of a bus shelter; it was funny, it was even, perhaps, cosmically funny, but their laughter was of another order. It was anarchic laughter, unseemly, crazed; they surrendered to it, having no choice; they were wet with it, streaming, exhausted, weak, spent. And still they could not stop. Once, as a child, S. Z. Hroch had been knocked down by a wave of angry sea, his mouth filled with sand. Incapable of rising, or breathing, suddenly aware that, yes, drowning would be like this, unable to rise, or breathe. It was—like that.

My husband used to watch me pull on my hose, Grace Craven said. And then accuse me of being provocative. I never could understand. I was just pulling on my hose, just getting dressed. She demonstrated, seated on the edge of the bed, skirt pulled up. Rolling the hose, inclining each taut leg upward, as in a slow-motion film. Hroch imagined her husband's gaze riveted to the unfolding drama. Imagined her pretending to be unaware, secretly performing this reverse striptease, watching its effect. Her white plump thighs, her damp flesh. Dietrich as Lola-Lola. Contemptuous. Her husband as the professor, mesmerized, helpless. Thighs. Why do you do that? his voice hoarse. What? Do what? I'm just getting dressed; idiot. Delighted by now with the proof of her power, exaggerating the pose, the being exposed, rolling the flimsy silk slowly over the silken flesh, pausing to look up at him, mystified, smiling, teasing. What? *What?* I'm just putting on . . . my hose. And he groaning, his own flesh rising up against him, branding him fool, unmanning him. She exultant, keeping her delight secret behind the feigned surprise. Really, I didn't mean, hey, I wasn't, what, come on, don't, I thought we were . . . in a hurry to . . . oh, ohh. And finally her inordinate pleasure in the triumph, the overtaking. Yes, oh. And half-rolled stockings stopped, midthigh, and he, groaning, and she, grinning. Lola-Lola writhes again.

It seemed important to make love once in the museum. On the carpeted floor of the Homolka archive, beneath the carrels, risking discovery by late-night scholars or uniformed guards, by Ms. Pfister or some other staff member, escorting a wealthy patron on a tour of the research facilities. Without this exotic flavoring, the possibility of rude surprise, no one would ever succumb to a whim of passion in that place. But they did. Grace Craven and S. Z. Hroch. The lamplight cast golden shadows on desktops littered with important scholarly thoughts. An electric typewriter, left on by mistake, hummed someone's interrupted song.

Hroch had stopped in to gaze at Grace's head thrown back, her feet up on the desktop, ankles crossed. He stared at her round coffee cup, her husband's big sporty watch, her stack of rough yellow paper. All of it seemed filled with sudden sexual symbolism. He reached toward her, hesitated, drew back his hand. Her eyes opened, as though he had made a sound. In an instant they were together, fastened, sinking down. In another they had ceased listening for footsteps, for rattling keys. No one came to the door. If anyone had found them, they could not have sprung apart, could not have moved. Stunned, as though from a blow. Armed intruder! One of them could have shouted, perhaps, with a distracted wave toward the sealed windows. Quick, after him! Perhaps they would have gone away then, the late-night scholars, the guards, the wealthy patrons. And left the pair of them as they were, furled, heaped, and streaming like bright fallen banners on the consecrated ground.

But by the following summer discontent had ripened between them, and changed form. The red maple that shaded Hroch's old summer house had been pruned too;

after his divorce, he saw it once, driving by; it had the delicate form of a young tree, a sapling—only a few leafy branches, struggling. But it was nearly a half-century old, and when he and his wife lived in that house it was full and grand, its shadow spread so thick and wide that shrubs and flowers beneath it never caught the sun. Grace Craven had come there once to stay; he made love to her on the bank of the stream; they had fresh blueberries bought from a roadside stand. On an impulse he dipped them in cream and then inside her body, one by one, and then bent his head and took them back. You are gross, she had said. Are you shocked? he had asked. And she had laughed, not replying, thinking that his wife and her husband were driving toward them; at any moment they would be here, must be here.

It was never any use hurrying Grace; she operated on what her family called Grace-time. Urgency was nervous-making; not for her; she rejected it as bad for her health, for her scholarly concentration. Pausing to smell the flowers was prescribed. Hard to resist such a philosophy. Still, Hroch's body had tensed with the effort not to run, not to cover them both—with clothing, towels, postures of innocence, words. They should be discovered curled in separate lawn chairs, sipping iced tea, arguing about the dead horse in *The Godfather.*

Still Grace seemed blissfully unaware of Hroch's distress; if she had sensed it, it would have merely amused her. On the whole, drama amused her. Or she wanted to be found like that, wanted to explode something—someone's life?—like a child with a lighted sparkler. Her eyes were mischievous; she was playing a game of chicken, as fifties teenagers used to do in their cars, gunning their motors, driving straight for each other, at killing speed. First one to veer off the collision course loses. Chicken!

Hroch heard the crunch of car wheels on the gravel driveway. He streaked into his house, scooping up towels, shorts, books, sunglasses, scattered wits. As he ran he heard Grace Craven's laughter following him like a playful, switching tail. Had she not heard the wheels? Of course she had.

Her husband spent that weekend taking photographs. Relentlessly, as though he had been sent by someone else to record all their relationships, disintegrating. He and Grace would have a nasty row, he would grow ominously silent, pick up his camera, aim it carefully at her, running along the beach, topless, splashing in the sea. He never caught S. Z. Hroch in a single frame. Not a trace of him, not a corner of his towel. It was Hroch's house, but Hroch was conspicuously absent. The record would show that he did not exist, only that Grace Craven frolicked there, that the sun sparkled on the water. Hundreds of photographs, a short history of the world. What her husband did was justifiable, of course; a simple case of self-defense, open and shut. Years later, he would have this lovely album. This was the time we had then, he would say. How beautiful it was, she was, we were, at that time.

It summoned one's gaze; there was no ignoring it, not even riding past, on the up escalator. Draped on a bored display mannequin, a blue mink parody of every silk dressing gown a film gangster was ever caught dead in. Not a dark blue mink; an electric royal blue mink. With great rolled collar and cuffs of thunderous black. Oh, it was witty; it was tongue-in-chic—in the way that only monstrous luxury can afford to be.

Try it on, Hroch dared Grace Craven, knowing perfectly well how the conceits of fashion enraged her. Silk jodhpurs, silver sneakers—she took such jokes as personal affronts. Worst of all, imitation street bums' clothes, carefully tattered for people so rich they could choose to look desperate.

Do you think the poor are flattered? she would say. That boy who sharpens his hair into angry green spikes? The skinhead girl wearing a live boa as a boa? Think they're amused to see two-hundred-dollar jeans with ripped knees just like theirs?

She would say.

Now, here she was, nestling into this astonishing blue cocoon, rolling the collar up to her ears, laughing with delight at her own startled image in mirrored triplicate. Mink fronted, sided, backed.

S. Z. Hroch couldn't tell which image was more surprised.

She looked glorious. In a bad-guy's bathrobe the color of, the price of, say, cabochon sapphires that carry an ancient curse. Her eyes suddenly matched.

He drew a breath, sharp as a cut. She glanced at him as though he had caught her in mid-crime. Then she began chattering, laughing, taking the thing off, putting it quickly away from her. Had she caught him thinking? If he had a fortune, would he have squandered it there, on such a gift, for her? Did she think he had a fortune? Did he want her to think so?

Yes, was the answer, both answers, all answers.

Let's go, he said, in a strangled voice. She sprang ahead of him, then whirled and kissed him lightly, signifying that it had been a game, didn't he know? They had been playing. Slyboots. On the way out of the shop, he saw her hand dart out and seize a crystal goblet by its slender throat; saw her sweep it off a display shelf in a single swift stroke, like a tennis forehand. Reckless. *Now,* did he see? It *was* a game.

Months later, at a dinner in her apartment, the goblet was set in front of him, filled with his favorite wine.

Her daughter pointed to the glass with a mischievous grin. You stole that, Mr. Hroch. Didn't you? she whispered. Mom told us.

Did she? Hroch murmured absently, raising it in a toast.

That was the moment S. Z. Hroch fell out of love and thought of how to get rid of the body. He would set Grace Craven to capture Magdalene for the museum. They all deserved each other. And he had nothing to lose.

Pasta of the day? Arcachon oysters? Little tiny squashes shaped like Chanukah toys? Ms. Pfister, lady archivist, sweetly says: Tell us who else secretly thinks you're as perfect for this project as we think you are. We need a voice that will carry, you understand, with the trustees. Someone who knows you are not a mere chronicler of

Linda Darnells. Not that we—not that anyone—ever thought you were. Mind you. But just for the record, now. Tell us who, someone wonderfully respected, someone august, who thinks that you are—who would say aloud, for the record, that you are—the only person who can deliver this package. Just so that we have a place to begin. Because, you do understand, we know that if—*when*—we acquire the Magdalene collection, you must already have achieved the necessary.

Magdalene needs to be perceived, reperceived, if you will, as the serious female film figure we all know she is. It will be a formidable task to erase some of the images . . . the upside-down one, that sort of thing. The public needs a cleansed Magdalene. Just as it needed a Marilyn to die for her sins. That white pleated skirt blowing up to her you-know-what. And the next minute, dead. Very satisfying to the moral code. What people still require of movie stars. Don't you agree?

Grace Craven was absolutely silent. For the life of her—for the life of Magdalene—she could not think of a single august champion. Who would risk a reputation to aver that Magdalene should be redeemed, that Grace Craven was sent to be her redeemer? *Can* you make a serious historic figure out of a floozy? Grace thought: If Magdalene were dead, would they ask this of me? Of course not. But the poor creature was stubbornly, inconveniently, foolishly, self-destructively, alive.

TELEX: Pollexfen/Star Immaculate/Limassol Marina/Cyprus

Any decision on the Magdalene? Looks no-go under a million two for it, bar another miracle. We want Craven? My opinion, she's the best. Requisite wide-eyed charm. Magdalene will like her—looks, voice, style. We play her right, she'll get us everything we need. If it exists. But what about price?

Ran, she can afford to wait us out. Not as hungry as some. Still, like you said, there's no prize quite like this. For Craven, Magdalene is it. The real thing. Which is key. Magdalene being somewhat tougher nut than we expected.

Hear Texas has some interest? Craven thinks so. Let's move if we're moving.

Hroch

As usual, the trustees took their time. Hroch waited. Hroch was out of the loop. The Magdalene story, search for the body, false leads, all the rest, was dead before Pollexfen responded, by Telex, from Kizlar.

TELEX: Hroch/Museum Arts/New York
From Pollexfen

S. Z.: Sorry not to have got back in time. Well, blessing in disguise, my opinion. Remember the Monroe. Licensing fees alone, once they're out of the picture. Speaking of timing. We stay lucky, Marilyn will have peaked just when we acquire Magdalene. Public already moved off "real" Marilyn to cartoons. Safer sex, right? People are always glad when it's over. Just like in the movies. They need somebody to tell em what really happened.

I assume nobody ever talked money with la Craven.

So. To make sure we all understand each other. There's a point in the life of filmic art, like anything else, where the "live" illusionist, including the subject —especially the subject—is through; it's history's turn. Delicate moment, this. Requires total control. Why I say we're in better shape than when this project first proposed; at least the subject has quit making rude noises.

As for competition, trust you can assure us no problem there. Know for a fact Texas had been talking to the lady. Possibly also Atlanta. The Modern?

Main thing now is reassess our position, light of developments. As I say, we're ahead, no panic. Shudder to think what we'd have had to pay for the Monroe if she'd still been around, full of tears, agents. Worse than the Liz mess. As I told the board, last meeting, had Liz decently O.D.ed say a year after Dick, we'd have got all the cash we needed for the proposed romance archive. Instead of no deal plus a bloated subject with surgical and booze bills up the old kazoo—and I do mean old, and I do mean kazoo.

So. Women do go on. That's our trouble. Contrary to the fable, live goose never lays golden egg. Or rather she lays it, but then she lays on it. So what she lays is an egg, full stop. Anyway. Craven. She's kidding about the million two. Tell her we want to do right by both of them. Low six figures, max. Plus flowers. Maybe a nice lunch. By the way, you catch rerun of old Magdalene chat show on BBC? Looking monstrous fat, hair like meringue on a pudding. Poor baby. Names she dropped, old playboys (*not* me), tycoons. One killed himself? One flew over her cuckoo nest every day, dropping emeralds into her pool? Never mattered which lies she told, who she did what to. She was always pure voice, delivery. *Almost* Dietrich. Though Dietrich . . . well, pre-TV. You could only have her do it to you at the Palace, not in your lousy motel room.

My opinion, the tack—tell Craven if you want—is that Magdalene was the last big O. Magdalene proved sex *is* death. Cold fusion. Solves the world's energy crisis, right?

Pollexfen
Bostançi Marina
Kizlar

MAGDALENE

He used to talk about the other one. Well, I did too, it's what we had in common. After a while, though, I really did wonder was it me he wanted to get into, or the ghost of *him*. What is "getting in," exactly? If nobody ever knows whether in fact you got in, except for the girl, and who listens to her, who does she ever tell? Well, some try. Sinatra said hell hath no fury like a hooker with a literary agent. On the other hand, once she's dead nobody can prove you didn't get in. Whereas when you do, when he did, it was nothing but Am I, I mean am I really, as good as the other one? Slower? Better? Really—better? How'm I better?

Well, I would say, you talk to me.

My father, he'd groan. My father said never talk to—women.

I know, I'd say. But your father was . . . all fathers lie.

My brother too, my brother said, Just talk their clothes off. After that, what's to say?

But you're different. Don't you want to be?

No choice. If I'm not, don't you see, then I'm nothing, I don't exist.

You do exist, oh God, you exist—don't you feel it? Now?

Yesyesyes.

Well, so, I was it, the prize, best toy, a live one to share, split, steal. Did they talk to each other about me? Or did each of them only talk to me about the other?

And what do you think I was after? Think I liked being the thing they fought over? I wanted the one. The other moved in on that. Full of sympathy. He understood. Poor me. He was younger, prettier, smarter. He was trouble.

I was too. Am too.

It was a meeting disguised as a social occasion in the form of a meeting. Like all events that are about money, it was held high up in a stone-and-glass tower, in a space made to look like the banqueting hall of a monarch.

Grace Craven arrived twenty-five minutes late, after several refusals to come at all. Suspecting, with her unerring gift of second scent, that it was a trap; that she would not emerge unscathed; men who chartered jets and limousines invariably meant to betray the person they were meeting. Nevertheless she was here, finally, at their doubtful mercy.

They were seated about an enormous square table elaborately set with old silver; heavy white napkins, starched and twisted into great V-shaped rolls, had been thrust into the crystal wine goblets like a flock of captive birds. Lesser white herons. Behind each guest stood a uniformed servant, gloved, silent, poised on tiptoe and quivering slightly, like a fine gun dog. The edges of the room were in shadow, so that the diners could not quite see the sideboards laden with rare and playful wines; morsels of exotic fish; dwarf fruits; death masks of leaves and flowers cast in whimsical shades of chocolate.

Each course was accompanied by a film. This custom permits comfortable silence, invisible drinking, and a temporary immunity to the harmful rays of hungry eyes. The servants served stealthily; no glass went unrefilled, no plate unreplenished. And all of it in the dark—secret gluttony, secret luxury, the very best kind.

The longest film was about greed and betrayal. A period piece. Grace covered her glass against the sound of expensive liquid pouring. One must remain alert for one's own betrayals.

The film ended; the heroine, played by Magdalene, died beautifully; men had profited from having pretended to love her.

Discreet lights relieved the privacy of everyone's shameful satisfaction. Grace said a few profoundly moving words to the gentleman at her left.

S. Z. Hroch's eyes flicked briefly about the table, avoiding hers. Coffee and sweets appeared; tinkling trays laden with liqueurs distilled from the bitter rinds of Oriental fruits. Hroch cleared his golden throat and raised a tapered glass of amber fluid. To our Magdalene! he said. And our Grace! He inclined his head toward her. She lowered her eyes, modestly. The trustees smiled their weighted silver smiles. Magdalene! Grace!

Hroch's gaze was now fixed upon the sheaf of papers

before him. He spoke rapidly. He could not in conscience urge the trustees to support the lady's request at this time. To do so would be . . . fiscally irresponsible. Although of course—he smiled here—the lady's proposal was dazzling. He had said so when they first met. When he had first been privileged to hear her views about the remarkable Magdalene collection. Prior to the inventory and appraisal. An undeniable treasure, he would still venture to say.

His speech lasted fifteen minutes. His gaze never shifted so much as a quarter-inch to the right or left.

Dazzling, he said again. Fiscally irresponsible, he said twice more. The rest was a blur. Grace rose before he had quite finished, and bowed to her hosts. You will forgive me, she murmured. I have enjoyed meeting all of you. Perhaps tomorrow Mr. Hroch will tell me why. I assume that, by then, he will know. Meanwhile, I thank you for this remarkable afternoon.

The trustees rose, unsteadily, exchanging glances. The lights were now too bright to cover their unease. Something wrong? Hroch had blown it? She was to have been prepared to negotiate. To do the job on spec. For the price of the plane ticket. No, she said. Thanks.

And then, quite suddenly, this hooked line from Rob Twist. The old baitcaster himself. Using his favorite flies —gray ghost, creamy damsel, hairy Mary. Guaranteed waste of time. But on the other hand?

MAGDALENE

No one here would know me by any of my identifiable marks or features—wicked pout, dimpled chin, remarkably prehensile upper lip. I may never again favor anyone with a smile. Even if I wanted to. My mouth refuses. It can't assume any human expression at all, not even that of a person chewing food. Meals slip in and out of place, I can't really tell which. If ever I recover sufficiently to dine in public, I trust the headwaiter will signal me when the sauce dribbles. As for closing weary eyes, shedding the solitary tear that speaks volumes, I'm afraid not. Perhaps never. Think of that! No sad songs. If I don't cry, no one else need cry for me. A vial of glycerine will do us both; we can decide that the scene should be underplayed. Think of it as deliverance. After all, a pretty face crumpling with grief, age, fury, crazed laughter. Wouldn't we all really rather not? And, look, lying here with my eyes open, I don't miss a trick.

How long ago was it I suffered the first unkind cut? Just a minute, just here, see that crease on her? What do you expect us to do with that? Cut! Yes. No talking, laughing, eating, thinking, dreaming. Just lie on that lovely naked back, staring at the dark, like a bride. Or whatever. And happily ever after, with a silver spoon applied nightly, to the laughter lines, and a hot iron in the morning, just hot enough to ping a water drop. Cutters and tailors summoned as needed. How old was I, thirty? Shouldn't have waited that long. Stitch in time. And it cures uncertainty. What the Mona Lisa might have meant by that expression.

In any case, as I was saying, you won't catch me eating in public. The way those vultures caught Dietrich once in Paris, scraping her leaking vichyssoise back up her perfectly unlined chin, into her perfectly unpuckered mouth. Which one of them didn't feel a thing? And wouldn't it have to be vichyssoise! A clear broth would never have made the supermarket tabloids.

As for my thighs, just for the record, I did refuse the offer, *and* the ten million, to display them ten years hence, or ever, in elastic support hose, for some scurrilous ad. Those will never be my thighs you see on TV. And just let them try imitating my voice. My breathless happy–birthday–Mr. President–Marilyn voice. What do you think they'd have *her* selling now, if they'd let her live? Memoirs, I hope. Surely not adult diapers. Industrial-strength bras? Memoirs are a girl's best friend. Never mind what the songs and the jewelers told you. Try selling your old stones back to them. Ten cents on the dollar? In Germany before the war, a Hope diamond went for the price of an exit stamp. Later it couldn't buy a cup of water. Listen to Magdalene, forget the solitaire, it's a loser's game. Save the incriminating letter, photo, film, video, phone message. Some day you'll thank me.

Alighting from the ferry, Grace Craven's first word to Rob Twist is Well? Rob kisses her full on the mouth, though she tries to deflect him. It is an old game with them. He beams at her, having won, makes no attempt to relieve her of her suitcase. She's up in Lavender Cassel's house for the moment, he says. I imagine we'll have to move her. She's not well, not at all.

Touch of? says Grace.

Medusée, he says, with unseemly satisfaction. Dove right in, minute she arrived. In the dark.

You saw her? You didn't stop her? Grace is shocked to find herself sounding less appalled than she ought.

I? Stop her? Am I my tourist's keeper? Rob shrugs. So, in any case, she'll be staying on. And the way it struck—he draws his outstretched fingers slowly, gently as a caress, across Grace Craven's face—doubtful she'll ever look herself.

You're sure it *is* herself. Grace searches his eyes; there are never any clues in Rob Twist's eyes. It's one of the things he counts on.

Sure enough, he replies cheerfully. And now that you're here, with your impeccable credentials, any lingering doubt—he spreads his hands, with a magician's practiced eloquence. Nothing up his sleeve. In his pocket, however, is a single photocopy page. He presses it into her hand. Go on, tell me. Whose writing is that? You're the Magdalene scholar.

MAGDALENE

Women never do die once and for all, you know. Not even the Madonna, who had every reason to. As for the whore, she has to be snuffed every year, just so that she can be resurrected, using only money and hair coloring. A harlot, like a Harlow, is not a live woman anyway. If we actually suffered one to live, she'd only grow old on us, or tell how her most famous client looks without an erection. Or—worse—with one. Her heart has to be stopped the instant we suspect it's gold. Then, of course, we can bring her back alive. On film.

Grace sniffs. Too easy. But she squints at it again. Can't tell anything in this glare. A lousy Xerox—

So here's what I suggest, Rob says, picking up her suitcase now. You'll have no trouble getting her to talk. Peek at the papers when you can. Of course we'll need a detailed inventory. Appraisers. But there's astonishing stuff.

I promise you. I've seen bits. Minute you have what we need, we can send for—your friend Hroch, if you like. Or Texas—whoever you think. Because of course you'll do the necessary. I mean you'll be sole broker. Lion's share of the—

Meaning you've actually got nothing better than this? She waves the scrap of paper, contemptuously. Ha! Not a shred! I knew it.

Rob exhales carefully. Woman's got no face. I told you. She arrives with trunks full of incendiary paper. Photographs. Diaries. Amazing letters from all the people we need letters from. Unmistakable. Handwritten. You said yourself—the bank said—

Grace waves an impatient hand. The bank never met the woman; it was all done with—

Mirrors and glass-bottom boats?

Agents! Grace snaps. Steerers! Pro and con artists like—you.

What made you come, then? Rob's grin is sly, almost nasty. It's two thousand dollars out of your way.

She grins back. Curiosity. Greed. Boredom.

Which of those was it killed the cat? I keep forgetting. He breaks into his sudden small-boy expression, the face of the adorable scamp that melted every heart but his father's; the one that always got him into or out of woman trouble, depending. Dr. Grace Craven, he realized with a delighted start, was still not immune.

That night, Grace wrote a thoughtful note to S. Z. Hroch.

Darling: Remembering our last meeting with much pleasure. Plans changing. Marooned here on Medusa for a spell, pursuing our mutual quarry. Are your terrible trustees ready *now?*

She addressed the letter to his museum office, in care of the Homolka archive. A calculated risk. She smiled, imagining Ms. D. Pfister's expression when she decided to ignore the PERSONAL & CONFIDENTIAL, and slit open the letter.

Ione Twist, at her husband's request, comes every day to visit Magdalene, to help with the chores and the boredom. Speaking in her best halting English, with the dazzling vague smile of one who apparently misses most of what is said, Ione makes an ideal spy. Removing trash, sifting it for useful bits of paper. She reports faithfully on Magdalene's activities: sitting for hours on her crumbling stone parapet, gazing out at the sea, scribbling in a notebook. Occasional letters arrive, addressed to "current occupant." Ione delivers these, pausing only for Rob to note the return addresses, to ascertain—the old roll-up split-bamboo way—what sort of statements are in the bank envelopes. He has a friend at each of several banks, in several countries. Ordinarily he does not find it difficult to dislodge information from bankers, using only the crude tools of real-estate advice.

Rob Twist is well informed about who owns what on every island off the southern coast of Europe. He always knows who needs cash; more important, he knows who is about to need cash, and what for. Over the years he has found his nose for other people's troubles to be quite the most useful of his attractive features. It is not a talent of which a man who once read classics at Oxford is especially proud. Still, an Oxford classicist with a sullen wife and two daughters growing wild; one with a failing café and an incipient paunch; one who wishes he had never defied his father quite so irrevocably when he was thirty—such a classicist, at forty-five, cannot afford to indulge his expensive distastes.

Magdalene's house has a telephone, a rarity here. She never answers it, in case the call is for her. Or is not. Still, messages are received. Rob Twist calls: Magdalene? You there? Magdalene? It's Rob Twist. You remember. I promised to ring when the disciples arrived. It's beginning.

She plays the message back, stopping at the sound of her name, in his voice. Not that he is anyone. But she feels the sound, viscerally, perineally. She rises to it. She plays it again and weeps.

MAGDALENE

Stranger called me by name, twice—a sound so exotic, like a caress, exquisitely tender (in the sense of pain). I cannot fathom why my throat caught. I am so tough that only the sound of my own name moves me to tears? Almost no one uses it—to my face—I've taught them all so well, and I call no one else by name; never have, perhaps never could. Except to say the word of some loved stranger's name aloud, to myself, as though it were a mantra. And I thought that was a habit I had outgrown.

Was it that only my enemies ever called me by name? So that when it is said I feel betrayed? Never had a charming nickname, some sweet, ordinary alias. And how I tried. Even as a young actress, inventing other selves, marrying, remarrying—change, transform, disguise, disappear—get away from whom? The one they despised? The one I would never be, if only I could escape. And now that I have—if I have—I seem to want them back. Myself back. All my selves? No—I can't mean that. I want—

She has always been like this. Voices, playing her, summoning her, promise and tease. Do they want her? Something of—from—her? There comes a moment when it no longer matters a damn. They play her with their messages, she plays them back. All are deceived, all served by the wanting, the being wanted. A young man slept on her sofa once—she does not recall his name, or when it was, precisely—but she recalls seeing him, towering over the other idolators crowded in her receiving room, the room in which she received the fleeting gift of their crowded idolatry. She needed his eyes and voice that night, and he, young, hungry, ambitious, was lifted up by her need. *She* wants *me,* he thought. While she thought: I am still I. Both were bent on seducing her, for their separate reasons, which were the same.

Magdalene has lived on, lived off, this interchange for a lifetime. He—whoever he, or, sometimes, she, is—shows her a good time in his eyes. Magdalene laughs, deep-throated, forcing the stranger to imagine fateful connections. The seducer, seduced? Both, both—and each by the seductive self.

In bed with any lover, Magdalene loves the beautiful voice that recites (from memory or desire) her beauties. Whether she believes the recital is not important. "Your breasts," says the voice. "How I feast on them." And so Magdalene feasts on them. And is sated.

In the morning mirror she turns and holds her own

breasts in her cupped hands, murmuring the words of that lover. Who's the fairest in the land? Who wants to know? Magdalene offers her breasts to the cool gaze of the cold glass. Say it.

Once, in a film, she was made to offer her breasts to the camera, to gaze down upon them tenderly, as though they were children or pets. They gazed back upon her, just as tenderly. Later, when they were alone, she played their favorite games, drawing wisps of silk across them, decorating them with sequins, painting the pale nipples with rouge and mascara, like wicked black eyes.

The next time Rob Twist rang, Magdalene answered, surprising them both. She remembered him, of course. The bar owner who found her this house? who had watched her dive into the treacherous sea? whose wife came every day to help, to spy? Of course. Come and bring the eminent film historian. Poet-novelist. Documentary maker. She would be delighted.

She broke the appointment twice, without apology or explanation, sending a note with Ione saying simply, Don't come.

On the third appointed day, he was to bring Grace Craven for tea. Magdalene did not send a note. She spent the shimmering white forenoon indoors, rehearsing. Without a face, it was more difficult than usual. She would have to rely upon her voice, on familiar gestures, on the fantasy life of her visitor. Well, it was only a woman. Chances were she was both greedy and gullible. More to be trusted, therefore, than any trick of memory or passion

Magdalene might otherwise be required to play. Greed and gullibility were articles of Magdalene's faith.

Therefore, when she heard the crunch of sharp stones halfway down the path, she rose slowly, confidently, drifting out to her accustomed place on the parapet, and turned her eloquent back to the sunset, as though the dying red hurt her eyes. She has always done this: the instinctive gesture of one celebrated beauty unable to bear the flamboyant entrance or exit of another.

She was holding, not reading, a book about the antics of English artists who had amused or inspired each other on this island fifty years before. In the photographs, everyone seems extravagantly lovely, the slim young men with wild white hair, the slender girls on horseback, with bobbed black helmets of hair like the heads of painted dolls. This one unraveled the sleeve of that one while he slept, according to the caption. Then she rose at dawn to cook the ravelings in a black sauce, to be served at lunch to the unsuspecting, sleeveless guest. How they must all have howled into their champagne goblets, when the goblets were not being used to cup the perfect breasts of one or another of the painted dolls.

Magdalene let the book slide off her white sharkskin lap. Footsteps nearer now, almost upon her. She rose again, suddenly, instinctively, hurrying to study her pale image in a smeared and broken windowpane. Will they find me so? Do I assent to be found so?

As Rob Twist started toward her, arms outstretched, threatening an embrace, she turned so that he might inhale the fragrance of her damaged cheek. The woman, Dr. Grace Craven, stood uncertainly beside him, smiling a wonderful smile. I'll leave you two, then, he said quickly. Not every day one's got a live sultan at the bar.

The women seemed not to hear him. Rob touched Grace's elbow. Shall I stop back, love, or will you find your way down?

No. Yes, said Grace. Her eyes were fixed upon Magdalene's huge black-mirrored sunglasses, as though she could see beyond the reflection of her own gaze to Magdalene's secret expression. Magdalene's hand flew to her temple to adjust the glittering frame. Grace nodded imperceptibly; a touch. Well, then, she said, to cover her surprise. Magdalene in the flesh? No mistake? It was.

Magdalene edged briskly past her on the narrow balcony, paying inordinate attention to Rob Twist's passage from the house out onto the path below.

He paused before descending the hill, glanced upward, grinned. One down, he thought. But not exultantly. Nothing, he well knew, was as dangerous to trust as a running start. Grace had options. Spotless reputation at stake. She was the sort that often refused to bite. Also the sort whose bite was venomous.

I thought you might like to have a look, Grace was saying, at some of my writings about you. In case.

The mirrors turned like spotlights. Magdalene took the proffered envelope. Not really, she said, however.

When I was eighteen, Grace says, I won a thousand yttria for a poem about this island. It was a newly minted bill with your portrait on it; I hadn't known there was such a thing. And when I saw it, I knew I would not spend it. I was sure it was magic.

Magdalene would have smiled her smile, if she could.

There was only the reflex now, an echo of the smile, a bad print. The crescents formed beside the mouth, the head tilted back, as though it swung on an invisible hinge, released by the sound of the flatterer's voice. Say the magic word, the word "magic," win a thousand yttria.

So, she sighed, you want the truth?

Of course, said Grace, I already have everything else.

Magdalene laughed impolitely. But she was pierced. Her skin was. Her scar tissue. Ancient aching child's flesh, that had always been anyone's for the stroking.

Grace Craven's purple silk shirt clung to her. She was in for it. Winning what she wanted always terrified her; she never reckoned the cost beforehand. Instinctively she shrank from knowing. Assumed the bill, if bill there was, would be paid by someone who could afford it, someone who would pay it without a thought. Only too happy. Someone who. But perhaps that wasn't entirely true. Perhaps she did know, always, on some deeply pragmatic level, that the bill would eventually be forwarded, that there would be no money to pay it, that she would be exposed at last: poor, uninvited, a fraud. I thought she was with you. Me? Hardly. Or not even a reply. A quizzical glance. A blank stare.

Which was why Grace always set her traps for the vulnerable: the once-idolized, formerly beautiful, poor little rich. And how they rose to her. How tenderly she pressed their rusted, secret levers. Lonely, frightened, unloved, forgotten? How can it be? Oh. You're teasing me. Everyone teases me. Don't tease me. Not you.

And so Magdalene, peering through hooded eyes, eyes of the desperate orphan child, must dissolve in tenderness.

Yes, she will say. Be in my life, take what you want. I have a fortune. Useless to me. Grace Craven will sigh. Disappointed, terrified, elated. Oh, God, so easy. How she longs to be caught. How she dreads, needs, to be caught. Stop me. Arrest me. Bring me down.

Now suppose I were to write your life, said Grace suddenly. And you didn't like it. Would you sue me?

Again Magdalene threw back her head in the soundless mime of laughter that had been photographed, holographed, silk-screened, reproduced on dinner plates. Showing only the long column of throat. Perfectly phallic, some said.

Sue you? she breathed. If I don't like it, dear, I'll have you killed. Whereas if I do like it . . . I'll kill you myself. I mean, why else would I let you in on my fame and fortune?

Grace fixed the mirror-shaded face with her bluest stare. Seriously, she said. Magdalene did not reply.

Not a tempting offer, said Grace.

Mm. Well. My first director assured me killing was the ultimate experience. He was very young at the time. Rippling with upper-body strength and hormone imbalance. But I was even younger. Smug in my imagined beauty. My power. I giggled rudely at him. I said killing was nothing. Giving birth was the only true act. Creating life in one's own, out of one's own, body. The *threat* of life, I said. That's ultimate.

What did he say? Grace had discreetly touched a button; they were recording.

Magdalene reached out and flicked it off. Oh . . . he took me to mean that I was pregnant. And fired me from the picture.

Did you believe it, what you said to him?

I'm sure I didn't. Risking life was what I believed in then. The jaunty assent to death, followed by the miraculous escape. Perils of Pauline. Heroine saved. Or audience lost.

Ah, said Grace, finger poised again on her recording device. Shall we, then?

This time Magdalene's hand, floating invisibly in its gauzy sleeve, deftly swept the sleek little machine off the parapet. Do let's, she said.

MAGDALENE

I can think of six powerful men, no, seven, who are beginning to think it's remotely possible that I may, after all, ruin their lives. Not because they knew me, biblically or otherwise. And it's not a simple thing, like blackmail. Not just some piece you once tore off, suddenly writing a filthy note to your wife.

The threat is that men who can do you real harm are going to believe me.

The real vagina dentata is the mouth of a woman who knows stuff, and isn't afraid anymore. What are they going to do, kill me?

They left evidence, by the way. Every one of them. They all must, just like in the movies. Leave the mark, the confession, the plea to be caught, exposed, punished. Telltale heart. Criminal returns to scene. Behind every cliché there's an awful truth, leaking.

Besides, without the hard evidence, they never believe they're real. Not what they *did,* but they, themselves. Why else would they keep checking their blood pressure, pulse, penis size. Number of times laid, number of dollars made. Piles of shit, sizes of piles of shit. And putting their names all over every damn thing. All their names—over my dead body.

Real evidence. Quantifiable. Believe it.

Rob Twist had left an envelope at the bar for Grace Craven. A note: Now hear this!—attached to a miniature tape cassette. She had to buy a new machine—big, shoddy, outrageously priced—at one of the harbor shops, to play the tape. But the instant it began Grace Craven's breath caught, in that mixture of joy and terror that marks the granting of impossible wishes.

It was Magdalene's voice, sounding young and desperate, the voice she had affected for *Ghost of a Chance,* when she played the restless shade of a murdered bride (not one of Grace Craven's favorites).

There were other voices on the tape, men's voices, one heavily accented, both rough, urgent. Grace had to play it over several times before it fell together with an irresistible logic. Then she transcribed it:

MAGDALENE

Please, can I talk to him?

I'm sorry, miss, he's—

I've got to talk to him. Please. Tell him it's me. Did you tell him?

I'm really sorry, miss. Really—

Tell him I'm dying. Tell him, if he won't come, he'll regret it. You got that? I'm not . . . not kidding.

I'll tell him, right away. Can I—I mean is there anything I can—

Just. Tell him. It's not a joke. Tell him . . . things he would prefer not to happen—well, they're about to; all of them. About an hour, I'd say. Maybe less. If I'm lucky.

Miss—hello? Jim, better tell him, someone's got to get the fuck over there. I mean she sounds—no telling what she's got—letters? shit. photographs?

Bluff, is my guess. They all do that. Remember the redhead—

No. Sometimes—this time—no.

Sparky, you an alarmist. This lady's big, the biggest, she's not gonna—fuckin' *movie* star's not gonna—

She is. Tell by the voice. They get that—Jim, don't

gawp at me, just tell—him, just send a coupla—send Vinnie to clean up, I'm telling you, we got maybe half an hour, tops.

Your ass if it's another redhead—

Yeah.

The thing of it was they cleaned up real fine. Except for the one detail. She was, I know for a fact she was, still in a coma when the ambulance came. But the bedroom, that white lacquer movie-set bedroom with the little satin mules with the soft feathers on them, like in one of those old black-and-white adultery comedies—well, Vinnie and the boys left it like a quickie motel room, sterilized, not a scrap of paper, not a pubic hair. Half an hour it was like nobody ever lived there, nobody ever took a piss in that crapper, nobody, not even the bim—the lady herself.

But like I said, there was the one thing, which was the ambulance coming when it did, so she wasn't, I mean you couldn't be a hunnert percent positive she wouldn't wake up. It was a little touchy, you understand. The ambulance guys, and the maid, and that shrink she called. Well, loose ends. Cost a little more than it should have.

But how do you, how could you be sure?

Never can be sure, doll. Just sure as sure can be. Five hunnert thou is usually sure. My experience.

God, Grace said. And wrote a note to S. Z. Hroch, to post with the transcription:

Darling Rocky:

I think I've got it. By Jove, I think I've got it. Look at this. Strong letter follows.

Meanwhile, study the Magdalene portrait on last week's *Life* cover. Does it make you think this? "How beautiful she seems in her dress with the skirt of white plumes. But *why* does she? Is it the plumes? The light? Her fame, her death, what her name conveys, suggests, promises? If I permit myself to become inflamed (inplumed?), could I find myself rich beyond dreams? Might she love me enough in one night to warrant changing her life, or her will?" Here's what it makes me think: "Could I find *my* life transformed, like the showgirl in *Glass Slipper,* on nothing but a pawn ticket, a beaded gown, a rainy Paris street, and Magdalene's face?" Let me know.

Love, G.

Ran Pollexfen had left Medusa abruptly. One of those endless, dreary Senate subcommittee hearings in Washington. Drugs, money, dirty little war in Kizlar. His name had come up. What did he know about launderers, Brink's cars, sociopaths taught to shoot through children, disemboweled victims hung up on trees with messages carved into them, like road signs? And when did he know it?

He was only a money man, he said modestly. They asked him about his houses, cars, boats, friends, income. He thought; he consulted his pocket calculator. Ten million a week, and change. Most weeks he had to carry about five in his briefcase, you know, for emergencies.

I've always lived within my means, he added, solemnly. Good-natured senatorial laughter.

Pollexfen was proud to be on the freedom-democracy team. Like most of the other witnesses, he thought it was too bad some people in this world still couldn't be persuaded to do the right thing. You can't buy 'em, Pollexfen said, chances are you got to kill 'em. My experience.

Not too many people watched hearings on TV anymore. A few bankers, a sultan or two. S. Z. Hroch put in a call from the museum, just to tell Pollexfen how great he looked, maybe fill him in on the news from overseas. Pollexfen didn't take the call.

Grace Craven knocks timidly at Magdalene's unlocked door. Magdalene has made it clear she does not like being surprised, does not welcome Grace's unexpected smile, her gifts of fruit, her eagerness to listen, if only Magdalene will tell her a story.

You again, Magdalene says, as though it were a greeting.

Are you hungry at all? says Grace Craven, ignoring the tone. I'm *starving*.

Magdalene waves helplessly, dismissal or resignation. Grace Craven accepts the gesture as an invitation; she leans against the door, closing it behind her, with a breathless little sigh. I've brought a picnic, she announces. We could walk down toward the harbor; there's a shady place, that lovely tree I passed on the way up.

No, says Magdalene, suddenly unsure of what she means to refuse, or deny.

Oh, I've disturbed you. I'm sorry—Grace looks crestfallen, bewildered.

No, Magdalene says again, but the word is fainter now; she has realized, with a start, that she is glad to see Grace Craven, holding that basket filled with warm, fragrant chicken and a bottle of chilled retsina. Magdalene cannot remember now what she had planned to do with the afternoon. This is how Grace always begins. She does not know it; she would deny it. Absolutely. Well, I suppose if you sat her down and talked about it, saying, you see? You did this, and then that; the person you did it to responded that way and then this, it is a dance. You are a dancer. If you said these things to her, she might very well nod, with serious eyes, a thoughtful crease in that wide, smooth, innocent space between them. She might even (but probably not) say yes, I see; this would depend on whether she was sure you loved her. And how sure. And how you loved her.

So it is really quite pointless to attempt an accusation. Grace Craven does not (she herself would tell you this, in a warning voice) respond well to accusation.

In any case, all she knew, all she was willing to know, on this particular afternoon, was that she had wanted to come here, to knock on Magdalene's door, to coax Magdalene into having a picnic. That she had wanted it to be a delight, wanted to make Magdalene smile and lick her fingers, wine glistening on her poor beautiful mouth. Grace Craven knew she could entice almost anyone into simple pleasure. It was a small gift, but rare. And she had mastered the difficult art of bestowing it wisely.

Magdalene, for her part, was not a fool. She might well succumb to enticement (indeed, she did so, and often), but whenever she did, it was only because the enticer reminded her of the wicked witch she herself had always meant to be. A picnic? No. But Grace and her gifts stayed for the afternoon. And Magdalene told secrets, true and false, just to see Grace's smile.

Grace Craven listened as a child does, or rather, as a child who believes in magic waits for the colored scarves to be born out of the conjurer's hat. Red, yellow, green, blue! Magdalene was no different from any other magician. Having a single rapt child, a glorious blue-eyed child, at her feet, made her voice light, made her tell her tale as though she had only just invented it—or better still, lived it.

We met, she said. I don't remember how. It was—she waved—no. It wasn't.

Nonsense. Grace stood up, as if to go. As if she had no taste for cat-and-mousing. You *must* remember, you know.

Must I? Magdalene demanded, pretending royal petulance. But she was already charmed. And Grace Craven already knew it. Grace always knew. But now she appeared puzzled; she stammered; as though she were uncertain. Most appealing. Well, she said, I mean it would be so wonderful. To remember.

Magdalene considered this. At least she appeared to reflect. Actually she used the movement to study Grace Craven, to appreciate the way her upper lip caught on the slightly protuberant eyetooth.

We met, she said, in my husband's bed. He was drunkish. I was boredish.

I don't believish, said Grace. Not a word. And besides, you had known each other twelve years before. Nearly thirteen.

Doesn't matter, Magdalene said, petulance rising. The man was ready at that moment. Whereas previously he was not.

Men, said Grace, noncommittal. She lit a cigarette; Magdalene seemed to frown; she snuffed it out. He was a poor baby, she said, suddenly. They are all.

Yes, Grace sighed. But so are women. More so.

Magdalene looked up sharply. Lesbian?

Grace's eyes brimmed with spurious tears. I need to know, she said, with obvious difficulty, what you need to tell.

Why is that? said Magdalene, now feigning boredom.

Perceiving a sudden danger, a trap, cunning, disguise, Grace hesitated. Then she reconsidered, honed, refined her plan of attack. Madam, she said, abruptly, what—who—*are* you waiting for? You can't sit on history forever. Daring the world to steal it out from under you—

Magdalene exhaled, tossing back her head in silent laughter. Someone tries every week. You ask me to believe that *you* wouldn't. Why? Because you're a woman? Because you're charming? Because I may be dying? If not of a *méduse,* or of love, then of the world's unseemly haste to reinvent me. All poisons are the same.

Grace shrugged. I don't ask you to believe anything at all. Of *course* I would steal your treasure. Though I'd do better by it than anyone else who's tried to seduce you, I daresay.

Magdalene turned her back to Grace. That glorious

back. So what? she growled. How *you* do is of no consequence to me. Only how *I* do.

Now Grace Craven laughed her most wonderful laugh. So, she said then, leaning forward, basking in the smile that finally overtook Magdalene's wary, hidden eyes. So you met on a friend's yacht, he spent a night in your cabin. The boat docked. You took separate planes pointed in opposite directions. Suppose he didn't let it go at that?

Magdalene considered putting an end to the interrogation. Rising, murmuring good day, closing the door. We met at a party, she said instead, without moving. He escorted me to my door. He sent flowers the following day, and every day thereafter for a week. Enclosing a diamond and ruby bracelet in each card. I kept two.

Grace sat back, shaking her head. Aren't you, she said softly, weren't you, Magdalene? *She* would never tell a lie from such an old movie.

Magdalene smiled a different smile. She was happy. The woman was skillful. The woman's knees shone in the lamplight. The woman was a thief. Still, for whatever reason, Magdalene sighed. The sound undulating like the slow release of contents under pressure.

Grace tumbled forward, impulsive, impassioned, falling to her shining knees, her enormous smile struck Magdalene's upraised chin. Sharp. Like a serpent's tooth.

Magdalene, startled, scarcely realized what had happened, or not happened. Grace Craven recovered herself, laughing. A month passed before she mentioned this incident. Did you know I was trying to kiss you? she said.

Magdalene took the news calmly.

Once a summer, Rob Twist does pig. An Aegean orgy of grease, sweating boys stripped to the waist, turning the spit, shouting, leaping, intimations of paganism, flames, the animal, fully recognizable as it revolves, its head, its blind jellied eyes intact. Paganism as interpreted by Brits on permanent hols. Think of T. E. Lawrence, buggering, being buggered, in elegant costume. It doesn't count, back home, if you do it, whatever it is, somewhere else, in disguise. Racist rapists in uniform at My Lai.

The historian knows this, and keeps it secret. But the artist, the performer, the subject, *is* this. Forever doing (or considering, or fantasying, or pretending to do) the unforgivable "it." Which is the mortal sin?

There is, at Rob's, on the day of pig, barely controlled frenzy. Menacing. Obscene. The palest swooping blond English lady tourist has beads of perspiration on her upper lip. Ione, the discontented native wife, who so longs to be English, to be not-native, reverts before one's eyes. Glistening with a film of sweat, her careful hair escaping in damp sinuous tendrils, eyes too bright, mouth too slack, Ione Twist wants, dare one think, the naked boy turning the beast on the spit, slathering its flanks with searing juices. Wants him to do that to her.

Terry Mould arrived on Pig Day. England's most independent documentarian, whom Rob Twist had carefully neglected to summon, had telegraphed his arrival with a package of photographs marked FRAGILE. HIGHLY INFLAMMABLE. It was addressed to "The Magdalene? via

Rob Twist." By the time the package reached Magdalene, some of its contents had been removed, copied, neatly replaced. Terry was counting on that.

Valerie Mould, his wife, had taken an earlier ferry. She was already at the bar, pigging. Rob Twist introduced her to Grace Craven. And have you written anything I might have read? Valerie asked. One of Grace's favorite rude questions: unanswerable. Valerie was one of the tall blond English; thin, angular, with that peculiar sudden forward thrust of the neck and head, common to certain species of wading birds. She had been pretty; she was fading into disappointment. I am a poet, she said, with an apologetic smile. A tendril of her hair fell forward, as though to shield her from an attack of raised eyebrow. My dear, it is for others to say that you are a poet, Rob murmured, but only into Grace's ear. Did your mother never tell you?

Valerie swooped and glided, in the way very tall, pale girls early learn to do; not to take up too much space or attention. Knowing their prettiness is fleeting, they seem to hasten its loss. Embarrassment of riches.

She slid into the only empty chair, next to a large, handsome man, familiar. She frowned, trying to think who. From where.

Yes, you do. William Hack. Used to be in pitchas. I just got here.

He is drinking lemonade from an enormous tankard. His hand shakes; cubes drop and splinter as he replenishes the ice from a bucket. Rob Twist winces, watching him, begrudging the waste. William Hack needs several tankards of ice when he is in a confessional mood. Women like Valerie Mould bring it out. Or perhaps it is just his sudden success in persuading his estranged wife to divorce him.

He is, he says, recovering from being married, drunk, and gay—all at once.

I had been having erotic dreams about your husband, he says suddenly to Valerie Mould. Finally I had a wet dream. Terrible.

Valerie nods sympathetically. Did you ever tell him?

Will nods back. I am sorry, he says. But as soon as I did, and he smiled as though he might be pleased, I was cured of it. Just like that. I mean the thought of him is unthinkable now.

Valerie Mould needs another vermouth cassis, her third. She never has three. Rob Twist signals the bartender with his eyes. It is too early, even on Pig Day, for this.

Will is murmuring now about his last date, with a Tory M.P. for whom he felt no attraction. They went to a movie about gang rape. And, during the rape scene, he fled to the bathroom to vomit. It was a signal from his body, he explains. No more sex; no more dinner dates requiring him to serve as dessert.

The cubes rattle as he raises the tankard to his mouth. Valerie Mould says nothing. This great handsome man, she thinks, with his lion's head, his magnificent deep voice. This man has led the cursed life of a Hollywood starlet for more than twenty years. She suppresses a sudden urge to tell him she might love him. That was what his wife told him, after all, and he loathed her for it.

Will Hack is dressed in his soft black leather shirt, open to the middle of his smooth, anointed chest. Men in the bar eye him with what passes for envy or disgust, although in fact it is a potent cocktail of lust and fear—the same mixed emotion he arouses in their women, in all women.

Look who's here, Rob says, with all the heartiness he can muster. Willie Hack, back from the wars.

A girl turns quickly, as though she's been seized. It's Hero, the girl with the scarred back, whom Will Hack sleeps with when he's here. Rob Twist doesn't quite know this. Hero, fourteen, is the elder of his two daughters.

She thought Hack was coming later, a week or a month. He never came this early. He had heard a rumor that it would be worth his while, this time. The rumor did not concern Hero.

She shrugged a smooth shoulder and stuck her tongue out at him.

Hero's eyes caressed everyone, but not for sport. It was the desperate flirtation of a puppy in a pet-shop cage. Read it as you like. Look, it loves me, it wants to come home with me, it hates its life, cooped up in here with those cool hands, caged in this smallness, those cruel bars.

See, it can tell, from a single sniff of me, how I would cherish it.

Please, can I pet it?

Better not. If you do, it will whimper when you go.

Hero is impatient with whatever does not pertain to good times, to adventure or pleasure, distraction from distress. She is a child one delights in amusing. Her eyes grow so round. She reaches up, flinging her arms about one's neck, crying out. One is exalted; one's footsteps strike sparks. Will Hack is as susceptible as anyone; it scarcely matters that he has played with her too long. Or that she loves his attention less now than any stranger's. She occasionally finds it nice that he occasionally claims her. When other claims grow difficult, troublesome, she is glad to think that Will will be here, sooner or later.

Terry Mould arrives with his suitcases, camera cases, film cases, a kiss for the top of his wife's head. Hullo, Hack, he says briskly, moving rapidly to the bar.

Rob Twist has just announced the next phase of the evening's entertainment. He will read from his new play. Followed by dancing.

That's it for feasting and merriment, then, Terry Mould mutters.

Arrest that man, Rob says affably, setting up his microphone.

The spits have stopped turning, although the plucked *bécassines,* suspended from their tiny necks like a line of hanged infidels, continue to drip silently onto the mattresses of toast neatly aligned beneath them in the fireplace.

Rob is still reading from his unfinished play.

Finally he stops. Well, he says. It goes on. Of course it's not finished—He looks expectant.

Grace Craven struggles to say something nice. But I don't quite. I mean what, or is it a fantasy?

Rob can't wait to explain: The last part—spoken by an old island woman—

Quite right, too, exclaims Tarik Pailthorpe, who has suddenly revived, looking like one of the Lost Boys. Not Peter Pan. He stations himself at Grace Craven's elbow. Not using this? he whispers loudly, indicating her half-empty glass. Well—But he has already drained it and moved away. She follows his progress down the bar.

What a beautiful head he had, long and sorrowful. He felt her staring, turned and winked. Conspiratorial, not flirtatious.

She nodded, without thinking.

Mm, I thought it was, very, Valerie Mould is saying to Rob. Did you say something about dancing?

Grace is still staring helplessly at the back of Tarik's head.

He turns finally and grins. Let's do it then, he sings, meaning dance, she assumes. He is swaying precariously.

By now he has had enough straight vodka to turn his eyes white, like the popped eyes of fish grilled at high heat. They have been evacuated, emptied of agony and intelligence.

She assents, following him to the middle of the room. The awful music causes large women in red to hold their arms up high, snapping their fingers and pointing their bare, quivering toes. They turn themselves like the animals on the spits.

Tarik and Grace confront each other like fencers, and begin to move. A fat blond woman sings in Greek, about sadness. They turn and step, winding themselves like watches. The golden beads of Grace Craven's sash fly in mad circles, catching on the buttons of Tarik's shirt.

We are attached, he says happily; we cannot undo it. Never mind. They turn and step. She feels the fingers of his hand, suddenly, on the naked flesh of her back; he has sent them there. She arches, crooks an elbow, slides her own hand back to grasp his, to wedge itself between him and her. Poontang, he whispers, with a villainous softness. I love you, don't you know it?

Poontang? she replies, tasting the word as though it were an exotic relish. What on earth do you think that means?

He is momentarily confused. You are too old to think so much, he says. His fingers are fighting hers for possession of the silken skin of her back.

They turn again; her flying golden sash is now hopelessly caught. Someone must come with a knife to cut her loose. He will not stop dancing. The music seems louder. Rob and Ione elbow past them with platters of flaming pig meat. At the tables, everyone is now nearly as drunk as Tarik. White-knuckled, both the Moulds clutch their separate bottles of pure water-colored fire, for dear life.

Grace Craven is tired.

Poontang, Tarik whispers again. Why not just admit that we are what we are?

The fat blond woman has stopped singing. The music, exhausted, pauses long enough to let Grace escape, pulling her partner after her by his beaded button, her buttoned beads. Ione saws them apart deftly, using a carving knife slightly stained with blood. Grace takes the severed button and plops it into the artist's breast pocket. He fishes it out and swallows it, glaring at her reproachfully. What does it *mean?* he whines. It *means* something.

She examines the beads of her sash. Perceiving no damage, she resumes her seat. The skin of her back is cool now; his touch has evaporated, like the life in his eyes. Men like Tarik, she well knows, are the dangerous ones. They have themselves been prey.

Terry Mould has moved into the chair next to hers. I

read this story, he says. Man moves to an island, undertakes an enormous work, history of the universe, something, years of reclusive study. Lives like a monk, thin, silent, spare, pure. Finally, he's ready. Knows all there is to know, not a word on paper, but he's ready. Everything there in his crowded, shining brain. Tomorrow he can begin—

He dies, says Grace.

Mm, but the point is, the narrator's point, the writer's point, is he's a success. Dying like that, dying there, dying just then. Spared the bitterness of an end achieved.

No, says Grace. Never read it. What island was it?

Capri. You think she could still hurt anyone? Magdalene? She know where the bodies are?

My dear friend. Rob Twist has moved decisively between them. What Magdalene knows is who paid the gravediggers, and in what coin.

Thousand-yttria note, Tarik shouts happily, from the far end of the bar. He raises his glass to Grace.

Have you seen her yourself, by the way? How does she—

Risen, Grace replies smoothly. She has that risen look.

I can't help thinking—Valerie Mould twines her arm in her husband's—of that former beauty queen who got into such trouble?

That sort never requires killing, says Grace. Not for that sort of trouble.

Terry looks at her sharply. You think someone might require it now?

Oh, Mr. Mould, sighs Grace. Journalists are such romantics. A memoir is not the stuff of violence. It reeks of forget-me-not. Untie the ribbon, it disintegrates. Pouf, the magic dragon. Or was it piffle.

You know, Terry murmurs, Magdalene used to call me three, four times a day. Toward the end, when she—thought he might really cash her in.

Tarik laughs rudely. You taped the calls?

Surely not the crying, Mr. Mould, says Grace. You did bleep the crying.

Terry looks defensive. At the time—

At least he never actually *used* the tapes. Right?

No one would let me. Otherwise I would have. No question. Anyone would. You would. He looks at Grace.

What about now? Rob Twist leans closer. Think they'd let you now? Who would? If she let you do the film, would you include—

Grace Craven permits herself a slow, confident smile. Well, *now* it's serious business. History. So to speak. If it weren't a news film, I could name a dozen actresses who'd kill for the part. Magdalene herself—would.

Everyone laughs. Well, but she's past it, though. Besides, she'll never, her face—don't you think? Rob graciously refills Grace's glass. Two lady tourists edge away, no longer interested.

And anyway she's crazy, sighs Grace. Murder victims get that way. It's in their best interests.

Terry Mould says quietly, Still don't hear you say you got the actual lady and she's got the actual goods to prove it.

Well, says Grace thoughtfully. Not positive. But she does recall a certain conversation. She knows a certain nickname. She knows why there's no J Street in Washington.

There is a pregnant silence. Look, says Terry Mould. I'm here to do this film. Frankly I need it. I've got backing, not in the bank exactly, but a commitment.

Poor you, says Grace.

Magdalene held the stiff envelope carefully, fingering the paper tape that sealed it, protecting her from confrontation. She remembered the brash young man, Terry Mould, wielding his enormous camera; its shutter had clicked like the door of a limousine. He had let her hold it, aiming it at him. She had peered politely into the lens; he looked silvery, soft as shadow. She thought ah, I must be lovely in this gray eye, just as he is. It was like an old person's eye, filmed over with cataract or sentimental tears. Now she stroked the envelope, as though it held good news, a surprise, her own face restored, or his face, making love to her behind his mask, his weapon, his terrible swift camera.

What had he seen, what had he done to her, each of them shielded from the other by this business, this game of arming and disarming. Oh, the words of it; here, no, up at me, yes, ah, there, again, like that, like this? beautiful, yes, ah.

Well, she still liked it, and so did they, as well as love itself, certainly as well as sex. It reminded her rather of the sex of childhood, the sex from which she had run to the mirror to see what had befallen her—what had been added or subtracted, gained, lost, irrevocably changed. Boys boasted they could detect the loss of virginity by the walk.

Girls fretted: *Can* they tell? Does it show? That I, that he, that we? Is it that line, there, or the stain of my skin, will it be there tomorrow, forever? A friend had sent away, ordered by mail, a pamphlet promising secret ways to Enlarge Your Bosom. And by mail the information had come, an envelope, discreet, like this one, containing a single sheet of paper: a crude line drawing of a man's hand.

Terry Mould was coming to make a film.

Long after the young man had taken those photographs, Magdalene entered a roomful of powerful gentlemen who once found her desirable. One of them she had desired; another she had not, but it was only the latter she had gone to bed with. Once, in a week in that city she had many lovers: A young painter with a wounded mouth. A famous writer who had risen from her bed after a perfunctory poke, and washed, and fled home to his seventh wife. And this man, Terry Mould, by then a thick, brooding celebrated filmmaker who had once captured her most beautiful self—all in white, with her heavy hair caressing her face and shoulders, her eyes caressing the viewer, the voyeur.

She had taken him to bed then to thank him belatedly for that luminous vision of her, and he had been tender, adoring, the best kind of lover. The following day she had worn a dress that seemed to suggest nudity; rude stares, flashes of light, the wrong sort of gleam in journalists' eyes. This thick man, this filmmaker, had stood beside her then, silent in his dark blue blazer with too much gold braid, shielding her from the consequences of her foolish impulse. His eyes shone. He was with her, had been with her, would never forget.

Now, twenty years later, in this room, he would embrace her, seeking her mouth as though to reestablish a claim. She would turn her head so that his kiss grazed her cheek instead. But he would hold on to her, murmuring inchoate sounds, for a long moment, and she would not struggle. His now-famous portrait was the woman they both loved, and whenever he came she would be here, safe, in his arms, and for a moment both of them would be grateful.

He was coming, he wrote on the back of his card. Terry Mould. To make a film.

Grace Craven had been pondering the ominous silence from New York. What did S. Z. Hroch mean by not answering her playful communiqué? Perhaps he had only fallen out of love with her. Or out of favor with the museum's trustees. Both of those were grave enough, and more than likely. But the most worrisome explanation was that for the museum—indeed, for any museum at all—Magdalene alive again meant the Magdalene project was dead.

In any case, Grace decided, she would have to send another, more powerful signal. Something to steady a slippery Hroch. Something he could entrust to trustees. Something even a Pollexfen could love.

Dear Rocky, she wrote. No. Dear Mr. Hroch.

> As you know, Magdalene is alive, though not well, here on Medusa. She has a photographic memory—

mostly of herself being photographed. And of course she has—she is—what is left of what she was. I believe we can produce a remarkable collection of valuable papers for the museum. As for the sensitive material pertaining to her celebrated affairs, the great men in her life (and implicated in her recent "death"), please be assured that her fortune is very much with her.

I am reminded, as I am sure you must be, of this image:

A wide street, empty, swept by wind, dark as a December night. A woman is hurrying, head down, against the wind. She carries a heavy parcel, a box that we know is filled with frightful secrets. She is very late for her rendezvous. She had tried not to be walking so far, in such weather, bearing such a burden—such an embarrassing, precious, highly flammable burden—which she knows will prove to be her fortune or her undoing; perhaps, probably, both at once. She had tried to persuade a friend to accompany her, to hail a taxi, a passing driver, any helpful stranger. She had wasted an hour trying not to be an hour late, not to be walking in this bitter darkness. But at last she had seen that she must go, this way, at once, walking into the wind.

She walks with her head down, body braced against the cold, counting the gritty echoes of her own steps on the stones, warning herself of the dangerous icy patches that glitter in the harsh streetlight. Then, inexplicably, a figure looms before her in the empty roadway. It's a young man, calling her name. She hears him calling before she sees him—white and black as an apparition, a bare-headed youth, holding, improbably, a gleaming bowl filled with pale, delicate flowers, pink and white, luminous flowers. Roses and tulips and freesia, shivering and bowing their heads like children whose mother has forgotten to dress them for such weather.

As the woman draws nearer, the young man calls her name again, now in a questioning tone, as though perhaps he does not know her after all. Nearer still, she searches his face, thinking he is not, cannot be, a real person, someone who knows her name, someone standing alone in the middle of this strange, empty street, at this awful moment, bent as she is on her dark journey.

He smiles then, and she knows him; he is the healer, whom she has never seen outside the magic white-walled circle of the room where he saved her life. Here in the vacant darkness, wearing formal clothes, diamond-studded, holding such unlikely flowers, he might have been death, she thinks, with a stab—she realizes, startled—not of fear but of pleasure. She stretches out her icy hand to touch the flowers, and he says, it's freesia, so that she will not forget to inhale the sweetness. It's freezing, he might have said. Or it frees you. She inhales deeply, then touches his paste-diamond studs, in wonder. He smiles, a shy, boy's smile, and drifts backward, out of sight, toward a waiting car, perhaps, or into a house. A wedding, he murmurs. Going to, or coming from, a wedding.

And I, she replies, am going to surrender my secret.

It was her only line in the film. It's *still* her only line. And I've got it.

Are you there?

Grace Craven

Memo: *To* Pollexfen
From Hroch

We still want Craven-Magdalene deal? Not worth what we almost offered. Though Magdalene won't put out for much less, my guess. Why she thinks she wants or needs money is beyond me. What do women do with money, anyway? Does anyone know? Clothes? Jewelry? They never buy their own. She'd blow it, more likely, on some—one of those Euro-hagfags who feed on crones to spite their mothers. Craven could at least protect our interests? Truly she believes, does Grace Craven, that she is driven by purest motive: the will to tell, to find, to discern, Truth. A game girl. But the task, in this case, is arduous. Possibly Sisyphean. What think you?

S. Z. Hroch

TELEX: Grace Craven/Magdalene

Understand you're the *historienne* intent on doing the alleged Magdalene. Good; good. She'll hum a few bars and you'll fake it? Happy to look at anything you find. Keep in touch. Regards,

R. Pollexfen
For the Trustees
Museum of the Arts

TELEX: Pollexfen/Museum of the Arts
Historiette.

Craven

So there, Grace thought, her cheeks still burning. How little sorrow and regret I feel. Relief is what. And anger. Bless my anger. It will help me run, for I have far to go, and heavy things to carry. The truth of Magdalene is very heavy indeed. I'm going to tell it, though, show and tell it, and somewhere I will be both honored and paid my due. I can use this rejection. It confirms all I know.

The cast, the island, the story, the woman—none of it, says Pollexfen now, versus Pollexfen then—needs telling. Not at any price.

Well, damn him, he is my benefactor.

And the rumor that she's here will cause a gold rush. Blackmailers, conspiracy groupies covering Medusa like a plague. Whether she turns out not to have the goods almost doesn't matter. She's as real as money can buy. Already there's a poet-novelist in residence. A filmmaker. Agents and hustlers. Some to buy, some to steal—or, if she seems in real danger of singing the wrong siren's song, to kill. Again.

She's a fraud, of course. But she's mine.

Grace Craven, arms looped with baskets of loose flowers and green, oozing figs, makes her way to Magdalene's house, at the sultry high point of the day. The island is perfectly suited to Grace's habit of sudden entrances and exits. No telephones, no distant early-warning systems. When she behaves this way at home, people sometimes frown or behave oddly, unwelcoming. Even her own family. It's a kind of carelessness. No thought given to what the recipient of her gifts, her surprises, may be doing, may wish or plan or prefer to be doing, when she arrives. But here she is with her armful of delights, so fragrant and beautiful, and she is so breathless with her gifts, fresh from wherever she gathered them, how *can* they resist such beauty, and with her wondrous smile lurking behind it?

The smile, the radiance, is of course the greater gift, her bestowal of self. Look, I have come, I have chosen *this moment* to give you something sweet, *my* sweetness. What? You expected me to come yesterday? Needed something of me last week? Not flowers, not fruit, but some service, some dreary chore, some appointment? And I forgot; I was thoughtless. But see, I *was* thinking of you after all, look at these, look at my face full of bloom. Can you still resist? *How* can you? I am here now, love me for it. Can I help being a sprite? Magic I bring you. And you dare refuse? At home, Grace's magic never fails. But Medusa casts its own charms and spells. As does Magdalene.

What do you want? Magdalene snapped.

Just to bring you these; I won't disturb you. I'll put them here, shall I? Is there water for them?

Of course not, came the voice. We keep the jugs filled only for emergency.

Pity to let them die, though; they're so lovely.

No response.

Grace left her gifts, wilting and sad now, on the stone step, in a patch of shade. She hovered for a moment, so that, if the woman relented, she would have a glimpse of Grace's shy parting smile.

No?

The smile wilted too; Grace Craven turned away, into the blistering sun.

The following day she reappeared at the same time. The flowers and figs were gone. Had Magdalene taken pity on them after all?

You? Here again? The voice came from another part of the house. Impossible to see.

Please, Grace said, and then faltered.

There was no further sound. After a moment, she turned away, this time taking the path upward, toward the old mill where Rob Twist lived. She thought she felt Magdalene's eyes at her back, but perhaps she only wished it. All the same, she walked slowly, savoring the possibility. Magdalene was not watching Grace's receding figure. But she was aware that the footsteps were directed upward, whereas yesterday they had gone down. When, later that day, Rob Twist and his wife descended the path, Magdalene was seated on her parapet, swathed in gauze. Who was that woman? she demanded, as they passed. The couple exchanged glances; Rob spoke. You mean Grace? American film historian. You remember. I brought her here? Writes about myths.

Myths? Danaë and the golden shower?

Rob laughed. Perhaps a *bit* more current. Great suicidal beauties, as a rule. Child stars who married sadistic millionaires.

Well, but what does she really want with me, this scavenger?

Rob smiled. You know. Whatever you've got.

Magdalene sighed. She any good?

The best of her kind. But then he shook his head, thoughtfully. An American, though. I would be most careful.

Indeed? said Magdalene. Why?

Well, Rob considered. For an American, truth is experimental. Unless one is extremely dead. Recent death being fit only for television. Never a significant amount of money in recent death. It's public domain.

Good night, Magdalene murmured abruptly.

Rob steered his wife down the path.

What was all that about? Ione whispered, when they were safely out of earshot.

She's intrigued by Grace Craven. What's it matter to you?

Well, couldn't you, I mean, if she is interested in talking finally, why not to you?

Because, he said, she's been waiting for a Grace Craven. That's why I sent for her. Perhaps we won't all be sorry —though I doubt it.

MAGDALENE

A private triumph, scarcely worth mentioning: I can almost make a face (what an expression).

The pain of love and loss ebbs too. One day, finally, suddenly, I won't feel a thing.

At certain hours, my face distorts; flesh knitting itself imperfectly, forming folds and ridges that do not adhere to the original design. The jawline rises sharply, then veers off course. No artist would accept the challenge; any likeness would be . . . purely coincidental.

The lines of old laughter are unaffected. Or perhaps I confuse them.

I sit with my face uplifted to the sun, the fine bones crying within it, complaining like unloved old people: why have you left us here like this? and I say to them, unmoved, matter-of-fact, as they used to say to me: all wounds heal; you'll be fine; I'm afraid you'll live.

Terry Mould is coming to film what's left of me. He calls it "an homage." Why not, I said. I don't know why. I never know why.

Not even when they gave me that first American award;

in a three-hour movie about an old four-flusher (is there any *other* Hollywood hero?) I was on screen, and in this artful dodger's life, for ten minutes. Six of the ten minutes I was stifling a farewell sob to him, over an ivory telephone.

My character was a kind of me—exotic, foreign, sexy—supposedly invented by this genius. He was a sideshow barker who could get girls to get boys into the tent. In my country this profession is still called something other than show business.

So the hero buys me low and sells me high and takes my money and runs—and I get to break my lovely heart all over my creamy satin chaise.

But it took me years to figure out what I'd done in that scene; how I'd conquered America. In six minutes I had proved that Yanks were the world's best lovers. Here I was, mysterious, larger than life—I was Europe!—made of molten silver and vintage bubbles. Dying for a red-blooded, red-necked, red-handed . . . four-flusher!

Sex was never really the point. Sex was just orchids, bracelets, fast sweet talk, and a girl dissolving in creamy satin and tears. Sex was what I did on the ivory phone. Anyone can do it now, in America, on Charge-a-call.

Tomorrow they're coming to see if I can do it still.

Terry Mould has arrived with his camera crew. Festooned with coiled black snakes like Laocoön. They drape their wires everywhere: garlands, swags, for a house in mourning. Magdalene watches impassively, her perfect nostrils flaring slightly, like those of an animal suspecting danger.

Each of them has rehearsed this scene a hundred times. Each believes it will change life forever. She will be resurrected; he will be reborn. She has an elaborate plan to elude him; he suspects that she will be sly, coy, difficult. He is sure that he will get her anyway. Each underestimates the other's desperation.

Champagne, she says, indicating the silver tray. He goes to pour it; she disappears.

Holding two foaming goblets, he turns to his cameramen. Did you see where she . . . ?

No one saw. She must be some—

Yes. Where *are* you? he calls lightly.

Right here. Right there.

Magdalene, he says, reverently, to the camera. She was always an illusion. Let's use some clips here.

The voice of Magdalene floats toward them. I was real, she says. I was not responsible for your inability to see me.

Terry's eyes roll; he signals a camera to catch the gauze draperies drifting in the breeze. There she is, he whispers. Go get her.

The camera's eye follows his gaze, the sound of Magdalene's voice, the flutter of sheer white panels.

When did you first believe that I died? says the voice.

Terry signals the camera to remain fixed on him. He begins to stroll through the shadowy room, picking up objects, setting them down, pausing before photographs of the young Magdalene, portraits, a marble head. He touches these things, caressing them.

Here I was! she cries. Don't you love this me? That one? See me then? Am I not exquisite then? There?

Before she belonged to the great man, he says, letting his voice linger over the important words. Before their love was a whisper in the world's astonished ear—

Too much, says the cameraman, under his breath.

Before that shimmering moment, she was ours.

Do you remember so far back? Disembodied laughter floats, Cheshire-catlike, over their heads.

This is shit, says one of the cameramen. We're wasting. She's not going to put out.

It's not about her, asshole, says the other.

Terry Mould gives them a look. Keep rolling, he says. Follow me.

The largest photograph, twice life-sized, shows her standing, in shimmering white. Parted lips, recently licked, wet, lacquered, swollen. Breasts rising out of the dress like irrepressible playmates. Her hair curls in silver commas around her face, as though to mark a passage from a classic work. It is the Terry Mould portrait. The camera stops.

Here she is, Terry murmurs, as we remember her. The woman we desire, the goddess next door who can make us immortal.

As you see, though—he gestures—the hands are too large. She always sensed that. Holding them so, to minimize them. The year after I made this photograph, she began to wear gloves. Lace mitts. Sometimes they shot her standing behind a desk, a table, cutting off the hands entirely. As though she were a thief—

Liar. Magdalene's voice is cool, light. My hands?

Too *large?* The gloves were *their* idea. They were afraid I might strangle them. She laughs, the full musical scale.

Rob Twist's shirt is badly sweat-stained. He has run all the way up from the bar to Magdalene's house, in the midday heat. Well, he says, the offer's come. Not what we'd hoped. Magdalene gazes at him with distaste, and does not reply, but waves airily—indicating the liquor cabinet, the bathroom. She will never grow accustomed to the unseemly haste of men in pursuit of money.

If it is not what we want, she calls, over the sound of water, then we do not want it.

Rob Twist reappears, not quite dry, pours two vermouth cassis, knowing she will not touch hers.

She is seated on her blazing balcony, wearing her striped straw hat with the brim as large as a beach umbrella. When she is seated like this, it flops about her in great waves, covering her entire body.

Where on earth did you get that hat?

What was it they offered? she asks, from under that hat of unknown origin. Mexico, she says, then. I've had it forever.

Seven-fifty, he says. A lousy seven-fifty.

Bastard. I thought he adored me.

Adored is seven-fifty, Rob replies. Hot for is a million two.

Shut up, she says pleasantly. Shut up and deal. You did say you could deal. Wasn't that you?

Rob Twist sighs, drains his glass, then hers, despite the melted ice. I can't get him up, he says.

Nor could I, she laughs. That's *why* it's only seven fifty.

Seriously, he says. This is it for Atlanta. I could try Texas again, UCLA. But you know—or maybe you don't—they don't have the prestige.

The cash, however, they do have?

Of course. But I assumed—

Never assume. Except that I do not welcome unexpected guests. Especially—she glances at his plastered shirt, his red face—those who come panting and sweating, to tell me what I'm not worth. Prestige! A million two!

Magdalene—

Mr. Twist. I'm afraid—well, perhaps I've come to the wrong island. Or trusted the wrong agent. Not for the first time, in either case.

Rob hesitates. Look, I'll try . . . another tack. But if—

Do you remember me in *The Devil You Know*? I was allergic to my husband. I needed passion, excitement, divorce. He gave me . . . hives, I think it was.

Rob laughs. You had that problem in at least ten films I can think of.

—And I asked my lawyer, What's required of a co-respondent? He said, The man must be seen in your house, with his coat off. Perspiring.

Mmm, says Rob. I presume your hives cleared right up.

My clothes for that film . . . sighs Magdalene. Especially the negligees. And the hats. I had diamonds on every costume. Discreet, ladylike diamonds—adored-wife diamonds. You know—S-shaped clips, a little spray of flowers, a slender bracelet.

You were idle, spoiled, and charming. God, I miss those wives. Were there ever such wives?

Don't you have one? Magdalene asks. Her Mexican hat brim has turned like the wheel of the sun. Say hello to Ione, won't you?

Rob murmurs something inappropriate under his breath.

And to Terry Mould, too.

That's another thing—what about Mould's documentary? He said you refused—after all that—

Leave the door open, Rob, for the breeze—

Damn it, Magdalene!

Her white hand flutters behind the hat brim, like an exhausted bird.

Stumbling down the rock-stubble path, Rob Twist curses, shouts into the shimmering heat, like a crazed prospector lost in the desert. He should kill her; if he had the balls of a Greek, he would. Steal her bloody papers, tapes, film. Burn the lot. Nobody knew what she had in those trunks. He could make up as true a Magdalene as anyone; truer. Get Grace Craven to verify it—hell, get Grace Craven to write it. Which telling of an old whore's tale was worth a million two, anyway? Nobody takes notice of who tells the tale. All that matters is whose old whore.

MAGDALENE

About a year after the stories started, about me and the president, I was on some chat show. The switchboard lit up with calls from women—all wanting to talk about adultery. Not mine, of course. Theirs. Women in their fifties, sixties, early twenties. Some had their first affairs in the fifth year of marriage. Some waited till the silver anniversary. One had the same lover for thirty years. My husband wouldn't care, they said. Wouldn't even notice. My affairs have saved my marriage. My husband's pleased—I'm happy; he's off duty.

Of course they screened the calls. Not one complaint about the lovers. I could have given them a few.

I forget what the show's topic was supposed to be. But it never matters. You're a woman, you're famous for being sexy. There's only one topic: Did you do it, who with, where did it get you, how did it get you in the end?

I used to play wild girls. Seduced, betrayed, abandoned, dead. Everybody liked that last one best. Then I played married girls. Tempted, nearly ruined, saved in the nick. Except in *I Confess,* where I lost my child and went to jail for life—without even kissing the rake whose house I fell asleep in. Never mind, I did lie down, and at dawn I went home in my low-backed silver evening dress. One look at the face of my baby's nurse, and the fact that I needed a bath before I could enter the nursery. . . . I was lucky they didn't hang me.

If sex is woman's power, in my movies it was always—only—a powerful curse. And they pegged me right, I have to admit. The kind who'll sleep her way to the top, if she has to. If someone doesn't stop her. But I was always (only) as powerful as the last guy who wanted me. Life imitates art, like they say. So I never got to play the Virgin Mary, or even Joan of Arc. But weren't they wanted by a powerful guy, too? The most powerful of all? Not to be rude, but immaculate conception? Somebody was sleeping when they dreamed up that one.

Grace Craven asks, What if your husband had lived? And you, knowing what you suddenly knew, and he, knowing that you did, what then? What if, what then?

Magdalene shrugs; Magdalene frowns. Magdalene thinks Grace Craven what-ifs for a living. Finally Magdalene replies: What if the girl in bed with the dead governor had sold her story, instead of taking a vow of silence and a house in the Dordogne? What if the candidate's ex-wife had sold hers, instead of settling for a TV series? Or that mobster's girlfriend who swore she put the bullet in her own tummy. With a rifle! And the drowned girl got up from the ocean floor to accuse the senator. And the president's son refused to get married on Gay Rights Day. What if, what then, what of it.

Yes, said Grace. But I was talking about you.

So was I, said Magdalene. And about the point where what sells papers is not fit to print. And the price that determines the point. But never mind. It's *my* papers we're selling.

They had agreed to do a series of pieces for the film quarterly, to be called *Magdalene Talks*. Scrupulously documented. Proofs positive. Collaborators.

Remember, Grace had said, your dying words about collaborators?

Mm. "My dearest friend turns collaborator. The one I despise dies for me. It's . . . vexing." *Saboteur*. I was in the resistance.

I wrote an essay about it, said Grace. About the logic of betrayal. Because of course it's the dearest friend who harbors the secret grudge. While the despised stranger, the one whose name you forget, has no history with you. He has only the envious passing thought: I could save your life. If I do, I rise up to your level, and bring you down to mine. If I die for you, I become the giant you were. You spend your guilty life thinking of me. So I win.

I'll try to remember that, saboteur.

Magdalene was studying her mirror, memorizing her mouth's reflection lit by the remorseless noon sun. How unfair, she sighs. Better not to survive; the price of survival is terrible. I mean look at that. Just there, just above the curve of my upper lip, on the good side; it's like a tic-tac-toe graph. I remember when I got that, parting gift of —God, I can't think of his name. I recall his mouth, however. No scars.

Grace Craven reached out impulsively, touched the spot. Magdalene did not pull away. Life is unfair, Grace said. A quote from JFK.

Let's see, Magdalene said huskily. You'd like to hear about—when the first lady made a pass at me?

The First Lady?

Magdalene shrugged, reached for her hat, disappeared inside it.

Where did you get that thing?

This? Actually, this was a gift from a lover. I remember the day she crowned me with it. A straw hat big enough to hide in forever, and a kiss that meant several things, I imagined.

Who was she?

Magdalene sighed. I was on my way to be interviewed, talk about my latest film, my latest life, the usual. As always, in such moments, the feelings are high and mixed, like a potent scent. Harmful when deeply inhaled.

Who was she? Grace persisted.

Magdalene went on. We were walking along an avenue with wonderful shop windows, distracting sights, brilliant sunshine in the cold, white air. It was our second-favorite walk, not the most fashionable avenue, but the one with the most surprises. A tiny shop that sold rare old buttons; a rug dealer who kept a pair of Jacobin pigeons. One pigeon had died; the other, grieving, had refused a new mate. At last, the merchant had bought him a mirror, and he had fallen in love.

Who—? Grace began, then thought better of it.

This day we seemed especially in tune with the street; every pane of glass sparkled with promises.

Here, said my friend suddenly. We have to go in here. It was a haberdasher's shop filled with cavalry twill and plaid woolens. Motoring rugs spilling out of antique steamer trunks. The shop's interior smelled like the stateroom of a great ocean liner, oiled woodwork, polished brass, and those old trunks sporting their stickers from Tangier and Darjeeling and Singapore.

If you hold one of these trunks up to your ear, I said to her, you can hear the sea.

The hat, this enormous straw cartwheel, hung from a corner of one of the trunks, as though it had been tossed there by some wicked adventuress, who was, even now, leaning over the first-class deck, blowing a good-bye kiss to a man she loved lightly.

My friend plucked the thing from its perch and placed it on my head. Look! she commanded.

I scowled into the glass. I was hidden; gaily invisible.

She smiled.

So did I. Then I hung the silly hat carefully back on the trunk.

We walked around the shop, fingering old-time luxuries.

Time to go, I said.

I'll catch up with you, she said. Her tone was mischief. She pushed me. Go on.

Of course she would buy that hat. She wanted me to know it. A rush of interior warmth filled me: an inward melting, like a sudden stroke of sun, or strong brandy. Dizzying. An expensive foolishness, I thought. I never wore hats. I didn't want it. I could turn back and stop her. I should. Really.

Instead I kept going—out the door, down the street, briskly; arguing with my unseemly pleasure, my unbearable discomfort, my squabbling selves.

Halfway into the next street, I heard her running, calling my name. I turned to catch that sly, slow smile of hers, which was the true gift.

An enormous shiny hatbox swung on a band from her wrist. I shook my head, as though to dispel the argument still going on inside it.

Don't you want to wear this? It looks wonderful with that expression.

She shook this ridiculous cartwheel out of its gray tissue wrappings. We were standing in front of a wineshop window. She adjusted the brim, studying me. We admired my gay ghostly image, stripes undulating in the breeze, like a huge top spinning over the reflection of the store's display, a pyramid of excellent champagne.

Where am I? I murmured. I've disappeared.

She grinned. Pygmalion might have had that very grin, watching Galatea emerge from stone.

There, she said.

Where? I said.

There. She was standing behind me, holding my shoulders. Our transparent reflected selves—giver, gift, given —met in the window, hovering over the holiday spirits.

There.

So, who was she? Grace whispered.

I don't remember, Magdalene sighed. I wish I could.

One day soon after that, Grace Craven stood before Magdalene, in a shy pose, knees pressed together, hands almost fluttering. Girl-like. The way she stands before venturing into the sea. Not the winner of Olympic gold, which was how she seemed ordinarily, how she liked to be thought of. Do you like me? she asked Magdalene. Do I please you?

Magdalene started. Suddenly Magdalene could not think of her next line. It was not a role she would have coveted, in any case. Woman of the world, man about town? But she was neither; nor could she play, in this story, the ingenue. After a moment, she nodded.

Am I different from . . . what you expected? murmured Grace.

I had not expected anything, Magdalene said softly. That is, I hadn't expected you.

It was easier without talking, one of the few things in life that are easier without talking. Some people disagree. They insist that lovers must say things, admire this and that, whisper yes, yes; or at least mmm, ohh. These sounds are reassuring. Magdalene distrusted every one of them, the entire script. Do you mind my not being slender? Grace said, with a disarming smile. Fishing. Magdalene studied Grace carefully, as though trying to decide. No, she said at last. I like the way you are.

I do too, actually, said Grace. I mean, it serves me well.

Yes. Magdalene touched her then. Or the skin of Grace's body touched Magdalene's hand, fused with it, as though Magdalene's hand had become as soft as that skin, or as the surprising taste of her. Grace Craven whispered things to Magdalene, secrets, inside Magdalene. They seemed to dance and swim in the heat, in light. Hours passed. I have to go home now. Grace Craven said, suddenly. Magdalene laughed at what she clearly meant: I'm afraid. What this is, how I feel, what it means, what will happen. I have to go home now. It was what a child says after a party. When the cake is gone.

Go if you want to, Magdalene said. Go if you need to.

Grace Craven stayed.

Magdalene's face refused to heal; every night the wounds would close, only to open again, like evil flowers, in the morning, whenever she tried to speak. If this is a divine judgment, she said carefully, it's a pip.

Grace Craven meanwhile began to sparkle and thrive, in a perpetual fever of delight. It's the life, she said. Meaning the air, the sky, the ouzo, the Magdalene. Working hard? Rob Twist would ask, when she stopped at the bar. She smiled. Astaire never seemed to be working hard, she said.

At last they had begun to unpack Magdalene's treasure chests, sifting and sorting letters, photographs, press clippings, film. Inventories. Donkey work. At first there seemed little of what Grace Craven had come to find. Only bits of any woman's distant past—the silk baby clothes, gold locket, tinted mother-daughter portrait, transparent lace dress once unwisely worn on TV. A girlhood snapshot displaying the intent, smiling Magdalene gaze, of a creature who can charm while not listening. The smile is here; the gaze is yours. I myself am elsewhere; do you mind? Most people didn't. Magdalene would not have noticed if they had. She noticed only the wandering attention of others. A star needs to notice that.

They worked together in the afternoons, as the midday

heat subsided, and before the water came back on. Mornings Grace Craven descended alone to the market square for fresh figs and yogurt, scrambling back up the hill, breathless, clothes plastered to her exhausted body, just in time to miss the last precious drops in Magdalene's shower. Wastebaskets and large pots were filled for emergencies, but there were few containers in the house; few of anything. The absent owner had paid her last visit to Medusa ten years ago; things in such houses gradually disappear. Except for the mementos shellacked to the kitchen wall. Stickers from ocean liners; wine labels; three-star restaurant bills; a ruled page from a child's exercise book with a single line written one hundred times: I MUST NOT TALK.

And in the courtyard, an old wooden weather vane: buxom woman in black, bent over a washtub. In the wind, she bobbed up and down, as though she were scrubbing, as though all was well.

The house had two rooms up, one down, with an outside bath and the strip of crumbling stone balcony from whose parapet Magdalene continued to gaze at the sea, at the large islands asleep in it, at the steep slope descending to the little fishing harbor, the one where the big ships did not come. Tears still sprang to her eyes as she stood there, silently pronouncing the names of what lay beneath her feet. Peloponnese, she murmured. Aegean. As though telling her beads.

She studied the young women with their arms full of bread and fruit, as they labored up and down the hills. That woman is someone I was, she thinks. Or someone I played. Maiden, madonna, whore. Who do I play now, if not all three? Three, equaling nothing more than one who's finished playing.

But here I am, still dreaming maiden dreams. Grieving madonna's grief, whore's remorse. And fighting off the other one—the one who can't be played. She's growing old, that one, older than the oldest man who ever loved me. Old enough to bury all my lovers who thought they'd buried me. Living past them all, past my past. Unthinkable! Turning into the nightmare, monstrous female who destroys the dreamer in his dreaming sleep. Men shrink from her; women are more terrified. They know she'll turn them into her. Everyone needs to kill her first. But I suspect she'll be—I'll be—the death of us all.

Magdalene? Grace Craven called. What are you doing?

What are you doing? Grace Craven would peer through the crack in the bathroom door, the way children do, or kittens. What are you doing that is a secret, that you keep secret from me? I want to know everything, see everything, own everything. But to know is not necessarily to own, nor even to understand. Once she turned suddenly, to discover Magdalene staring into her silver hand mirror. Not to make any useful correction, nor to admire the image. She did this often, as an exercise; it was almost a trance state, an extreme form of concentration, a loss of self. Magdalene had not sensed Grace Craven's eyes upon her, so fixed was her gaze. When Grace said, What are you doing? her body tensed, an animal fear, invisible hairs rising. The shock of sound, of invasion, made her drop the glass. Then, with a rush of anger: I have a right to stare into a mirror. It is a thing I do, it helps me.

Grace Craven laughed then, uneasily, Magdalene could not tell why, or could not bear to know. She was shaken, though; after this, even when alone, she could not glance at any mirror without hearing the echo of Grace Craven's whispered intrusion: *What are you doing?* Grace had not meant to break anything important. Perhaps it wasn't important. So Magdalene told herself.

Grace was learning her subject well. And Magdalene had begun to long for that—to be memorized, to be engraved upon Grace's mind like a cherished line of poetry, or the first image of Magdalene herself on a screen, that profile, those shoulders, etched against a flashing sea.

Grace Craven uncovered secrets of Magdalene that no one had ever seen, and pronounced them beautiful. Magdalene did not believe that they were, nor that Grace thought so. Still, something was beautiful about her saying it, and after a while, Magdalene had learned not to think about it, only to listen, to accept the saying for a kind of truth.

But she did not tell Grace Craven what she was doing, gazing into the silver glass. Did not tell her that she was replaying her favorite scene: the lover appears silently behind her, and stands, gazing at Magdalene's shoulders as she gazes into her glass, absorbed in her powderings and paintings. She wants not to know (or to let him know that she knows) he is there, until he makes a sudden gesture or sound, sliding the slender box from within the breast pocket of his coat, withdrawing from it the strand of emeralds, clasping it about Magdalene's throat, bending over her.

Had she played the scene well? A hundred times? Had anyone played it so well—played it as though it were as real as the emeralds? The man loves the woman, the jewel is splendid, she touches it lightly, then turns her radiant face up to his kiss. Darling, one of them says. Darling, says the other.

Darling, Grace says brightly, a few days later. It was dusk. I'm just off to the bar; Rob Twist has a message. I'll be—let's watch you in *Guilty!* later. Let's watch it in bed. Want to?

She was wearing a white sweater of Magdalene's, her arms bare, always such a delectable sight, Magdalene thinks; a sudden revelation. As a rule, Grace Craven disguises herself, making her body larger, in loose sweaters, work shirts. Then, by magic, she is delicate, slender-waisted: the color of her skin, lightly touched by sun, incomparable. Almost peach. Almost satin, the gleam of it. Warm to the touch, or cool. Both at once. Satin worn close to the body. Bare arms, in Magdalene's sweater, which she hasn't asked to borrow.

Magdalene thinks: What is her haste to be gone from me, to run down the darkening hillside to the bar, where the serious drinkers are, the men who come early and stay till closing time? Her haste, her light laughing; unseemly, really. She is merely excited by the darkening sky, Magdalene tells herself. Grace is a child in this way, thrilled by the little lights on strings blooming in the trees around the tavernas; she needs the cooling breeze and the violet shadows dancing on the whitewashed houses. Magdalene understands, she thinks, but really she does not. She shakes off the thought of abandonment and the second, impossible thought of going to join her, surprising her, all of them. Instead of nursing her grievance here, alone, on this parapet, with this solitary glass of nepenthe, counting stars in this solitary sky, gathering the darkness and silence around her like a cold embrace.

All right, she sighs. Let Grace Craven go to the bar, stretch out her bare arms, twist her gleaming shoulders, so that passing glances drift gently over her breasts, snug in their borrowed finery. Not immodest breasts, but present; breasts that are merely innocent bystanders, out for an evening stroll. And what will she tell of me? Magdalene? she will say, if anyone should ask, Magdalene is a mystery.

I wonder when she tried it on, that sweater of mine; when she discovered how it transformed her, so that she could not wait to wear it, test its effect. Not its effect on me, of course. Have I already ceased to be the magical snake that required charming?

Or was she merely compiling footnotes for the text? That portrait painter, hoarding his scandalous old sketches of me, in case they're worth enough to pay off his bar bill. And looking for Willie Hack. I know he is here, terrified of seeing me—I might indeed be me. He and I sailed here once, fishing for sea urchins. Before I became one. I was, we were both, in love with his voice. We stayed in the old castle, high in the hills. I rode through town bareback, astride; shocking the villagers. Or perhaps it was only a movie.

I was here when Rob Twist opened that bar. Someone like him, anyway. Some island bar. Outcast with a lovely native girl. Wearing their naked golden children festooned about their necks. Poor fish, island-fevered, wife gone all sullen, daughters growing wild . . . wasn't it the plot of *Tornado?*

Then who am I playing now, here? Ghost of a profile etched on a note, in a currency no longer used. The one who should have drowned.

It would be pitch dark by the time I began my descent to the bar. Threading my blind way, with my perfect sense of indirection. Searching vainly for landmarks—on the left, about ten minutes down, a long white house with an explosion of bougainvillea spattered along a blank white wall. In about twenty minutes, a space large enough to be a crossroads, if there were roads, if they crossed. A family sits on their front steps there every evening, awaiting the sunset. The old man in freshly ironed American pajamas, the women chattering, their laughter buzzing around his eyes and ears like flies on a weary horse. But it would be too late; even if I were at the right house, even if they still lived there, they would have gone inside. Lost in the darkness, circle and swoop. Cats watching me, faintly amused, refusing to advise.

If I went too far, I could find the way back from the harbor. At the water's edge I could say Bar, someone would point to it.

An hour, two; time passes. Grace is not here. She has forgotten the time. She is having another time. Like the struggling dancer I played too many times. About to be discovered, destined for stardom, but only if I ditch my old partner. He was always as washed up as I am now. We both knew it. But if I left him, the audience would hate me for it. Poor fellow had to read the message in his own eyes. They only want a single. He says that line so bravely. Take it, he says. You were born for it; I love you.

No! I won't go! (That was my line.) Fighting my tears, my destiny. But my feet already tapping; I couldn't help it. Dying to move on, out of that dreary dressing room, away from that lover, that loser of mine. Why am I playing his part? How did Grace Craven steal mine?

The bar would be overflowing, lively as a Paris café. Even the outside tables, the yard Rob says he's going to spruce up when the money rolls in, from some sultan, some mysterious consortium. Sale of the sensational Magdalene collection. He'll put in shrubs and lights; a fountain; new tables under smart square market umbrellas. Paving over the rubble, eviction of a hundred scruffy cats. The cats have always believed, like Rob Twist, that money is coming, and decent food, any day, any minute now. Making do, meanwhile, hanging on. Like the rest of Medusa.

And there's Grace Craven, I see her perched on the edge of a chair, sharing it with Terry Mould, leaning across him. The painter on her other side, stirring bitters into everything. Much laughter, some of it kind. Hers lifting above the rest. I approach them; she glances up, makes no other motion. Hello, look, I've come, I say. I am here. It's Magdalene! someone would whisper, pointing into the smoke. Well. As I was saying—Willie Hack, not looking at me, spinning an old yarn. Show business, cops and robber barons, dead bodies, money, sex, bought silences. It's a true story. I should know.

I can see Grace, entranced; she has a way of lighting her smile at the outer corners, so the full warmth of it curls slowly toward the center, as though she herself needs to taste it before offering it to strangers. When it finally catches, lighting her face, people lean into the glow like flowers or doomed insects, unaware that they have been physically moved and changed.

The public always loved it when I did that trick. Did they feel the same hunger, the same rage? Did they think: Why is that look for him, not for me? Or: How can she do that, when I never could? Thou shalt not covet. Oh, but however not? It's only a smile, only food and water, only light and air. I see myself edging in, ignoring the stares, the whispers. Is that Terry Mould? Beckoning, pleading with his eyes? Or does he only shift in his chair, not expecting me, not inviting. I approach. Terry Mould leans forward, around me . . . for a clearer view of Grace Craven's smile. She too has a tale to tell, a spell to weave. All about Magdalene. Willie Hack's spectacular voice and hers mingle in the warm air like the favorite lovers' duet from an opera one knows by heart. The words are lost; the music vibrates inside one's listening body. Did you want . . . to see my film? I hear myself saying. Aloud; too loud. See my hand on her bare, gleaming arm. She turns toward me, astonished. A claim? Have I dared assert—what? That I need? That I, that we—? And how does she feel about that? She laughs, the pure, delighted laugh of a child suddenly distracted by her bright, forgotten balloon, the red one. Of course! she cries. *Guilty!* Magdalene's old film, she explains. I'd almost forgotten.

What would it signify if she disengaged Terry Mould's encircling arm, and rose to follow me? I don't turn to count the amused glances fastened to our departing backs. Later, when I recover from this extraordinary triumph, I understand how Grace, in that framed instant, became twice as fascinating a figure. Which was why she granted me my victory.

Magdalene peers into the depths of her glass. Perhaps one more of these before . . . and then *Guilty!* In bed. Alone.

Grace Craven burst in just in time for the titles. Colorized? she cried. How can you bear it? Look at you, in relentless royal screaming blue! Look at that tufted satin bed; they've dyed it to match. And the whites of your eyes are flesh color. They don't seem to know where the skin stops. Oh, God, mustard yellow? For the hunt ball?

Do turn if off, Magdalene. Let's watch *Golden Empress.* You were a magnificent china doll. In your cheongsam. With your eyelids taped. . . .

Magdalene laughed, and forgave Grace Craven almost everything she had imagined.

After a while she said, Shall I tell you a story? About the president? would you like that?

Mm, said Grace, not too eagerly, not reaching for the notebook.

About that time, said Magdalene, when we'd escaped from Pollexfen's yacht at Limassol . . .

Mm, said Grace, more languidly still.

We were quarreling, passing a fur shop. Possibly it was a terminal quarrel. Now he wanted to buy me a gift.

Farewell peace offering, I assumed. He never bought gifts, never understood gifts, disdained the custom of gifts—except when they were bestowed on him. Then he weighed them and found them wanting. Like the givers. Not *my* gifts, to be sure. Mine he treasured, trusting as a child whose mother must surely know his needs, his size, his secret wishes. A child whose mother will lay the new shirt, trousers, underwear upon the radiator, so they'll be warm in the chilly morning, comfortable as hugs. Once he told me his mother had done just that, and in the morning the buttons, the zippers had grown so hot they burned him. Another gift found wanting.

Still, he understood that *I* might be susceptible. Christmas would come. My birthday. This time he would be ready. Please, he said. I want to.

All right, I said. Rather than Why, or Why now, or Why this, or No.

Fat, smiling, the owners of the fur shop bowed and brought jackets, coats. Special prices, they whispered urgently, proffering wine from a decanter on a silver tray. Americans, they said, nodding, gesturing, stroking their wares. Didn't recognize either of us. Only one Secret Service man outside, in a tourist's T-shirt. Cyprus is for lovers, it said.

The shop owners would come to America at Christmas, bearing a perfect gift, perfectly made, sleeves , trimmings, all would be done, anything, perfect.

More wine?

I watched him sip their wine; watched him grow expansive; happy to be here, selecting a perfect gift for me. Anything.

They would give a lamb jacket, free, extra, the men

whispered, still more urgently. If only we would order this coat. Or that. He looked at me eagerly. The great bargain hunter. This one? he pleaded. That one? Please like something I can give you. Let me buy you—

Buy *me?* I echoed. But I stood there. I slid my hands into this one and that one. The light in the shop had an ice-blue cast; it made the pelts shine bright as the owners' eyes. They stroked the sleeves, as though coaxing them to behave. I stared at the men, at me, at the furs. Coats for wives, mistresses, from loving husbands, guilty lovers. Coats to be worn in distant cities. With high-heeled shoes and handbags that would snap smartly, decisively. Handbags filled with money and secrets.

More wine?

So friendly, so skillful, such ice-blue chilly light.

All right, I said wearily. That one.

He smiled at the merchants. You remember that smile.

We would meet in America. I would be happy. We must take the jacket now. Duty free.

He smiled again. He had done something for me, won something from me. Duty free.

At Christmas the Cypriot Greeks came, bearing my gift. Bearing fur. Fur-bearing. I refused the coat. Ill fitting, I said. A fur coat? I would never wear such a thing.

They refused to return the deposit.

You'll keep the jacket? he sent a messenger to say. It must be worth something.

All right.

I wore it once, the poor lamb, staring at my reflection in car windows. I was meeting his brother for lunch.

That doesn't look like you, his brother said.

I took off the jacket and carried it home, tenderly, like a run-over pet.

The wind rose; I shivered in my cotton sweater.

I never wore the thing again. But it was important. It was what gave me the idea. Never again accept a parting gift. Nor any other kind of gift, but one. Something, well, how to put it? Intimate. Something only you can give me. Something money can't buy. Something you've given me anyway. Loads of times.

What was it? Grace Craven whispered.

Tell you sometime, said Magdalene, feigning her half-asleep voice. Remind me . . . She trailed off, adrift upon the gentle lapping current of Grace Craven's neaping tide. Thinking half thoughts of trust, of mistrust. Did Grace want her life, not only to tell but to own, more than either of them wanted the other? It made a kind of sense; after all, Grace Craven would at least know what to make of it. Men—even Willie Hack—had never taken ordinary comfort from Magdalene. Only possession. Like her lover in that horrid French film *Vacance,* walking behind her, raising her skirt to expose her to strangers.

In the night, in an act of silent love, Magdalene sobbed aloud. This was not ordinary weeping, though tears came. It was as if Magdalene's body had been seized and flung from within. Filled and violently emptied, as though she had conceived and aborted, all at once. The sobbing was involuntary, inexplicable. It stopped as suddenly as it had begun. Studying her, at first with alarm, then with amazement, Grace Craven whispered, What is it? Why? Magdalene had no reply.

The next time, or the time after that, Grace burst into

sudden, copious tears. Magdalene said nothing; she knew that another theft had occurred. Grace Craven had touched a secret, and stolen it. Grace's tears were an echo, perhaps an homage. But Magdalene's body grew thoughtful. She could be summoned again, perhaps. But her body, keeping its counsel, would never again sob aloud.

Before dawn, Grace Craven crept out to Magdalene's moonlit balcony, to write in her notebook. This was not the notebook she used in the daytime when Magdalene might peer over a shoulder, demand to see a line, amend a phrase. In the daytime, Magdalene would rise up suddenly, overcome by a whim, a memory. Time to study an old photograph: Do you recognize this me? I mean—my hair, of course, but do I still, am I at all—?

Oh, God, Magdalene, don't. Grace Craven never said this aloud. Nor this: Magdalene, shut up, will you? I have a thought, a doubt, a point. Let it go.

In the daytime Grace was part amanuensis, part Ouled Naïl—legendary nomad maiden who wanders the desert, serving the chance desire of any wayfarer. In the daytime Grace knew the purpose of her journeying. Magdalene was both the wayfarer and the way.

But in the night notebooks, Grace followed another path. She called these books *Saboteur*. They were to form the basis of her real work on Magdalene.

SABOTEUR

Magdalene is facing the end of life. Well, not Life. Merely life as Magdalene. The effect of her glance upon others is unexpected now, puzzling to her. As though she had awakened in a strange place, not having left home. What is it we have to say to her? We no longer speak to her in her language; yet our voices, our written signs are the same; in fact the people do not appear to be foreign; it is she who is foreign to herself. The estrangement occurred suddenly. Before the *méduse*. One day, suddenly. She ran to her mirror, squinting the objective squint with which she had always addressed her image. Nothing amiss. No sudden port-wine stain upon the perfect brow, no alteration of features. She smiled as though to reassure the mirror, rather than her own imprisoned face.

Leaning over my shoulder, Magdalene asks: How will you end my life? End it? I am not even sure how to middle it, I say lightly. Yet the magic word was "it." If it is an it, the Magdalene will surely have a middle, if not an end. All historians, all historical subjects, have middles, which we contemplate obsessively with due and solemn awe.

We need, I told her, to decide about showing "it" to S. Z. Hroch. How cool the idea of "it" grows, once it seems destined to leave my hot hands. Someone else's eyes, fingers, thoughts will change it, understand or think he understands, that the Magdalene is real now, a piece of work, not life. Magdalene says: Will it make me angry? Yes, I answer. Quite. So I too have begun to collaborate, to turn collaborator, just as I warned her I would. Until now I was its conscience, its prisoner. Now we are all in "it" together. God help us.

But for the moment we are still dancing. She and I with my words between us; I am an uncertain beau caught between debutantes. They are all dressed up and I, trembling with excitement, touch them with my eyes, my damp fingers. I steer them gently to a shaded corner, beside the potted palm, where we may sit for a while, get to know one another. They are, they seem to me, beautiful. Rare and glowing with the truth of Magdalene. I am filled with her in every pore. I have never been so filled. My body swells, as in a pregnancy; I bear a weight of emotion. No longer sure whether it is mine or hers, or a living thing separate from either of us. The romance of the romance.

Her eyes glitter like marcasite, faceted, the color of gunmetal. Set in her poor mask like chips, hard, bright, not of appreciative value, but of a material that regularly recurs in fashion, when times are hard and genuine treasure rare.

She turns them toward you; she adjusts them. You may believe she is paying attention. But she darts away like an insect. She cannot, in fact, pay any such inordinate price as attention.

The shock of the past is the real thing, all she has. Beyond the final glimpse of her ruined face, for the ghoul diggers, necrophiles, nostalgics. She hasn't been photographed in years; the old images, moving and still, remain the stuff of masturbatory fantasy now and forever. Yet we lust for the ruined face, it will be the ultimate object lesson, morality tale, caution: You will not always be as you are. Just wait: you too will be ugly and undesired. Her father, who deserted his family before Magdalene was born, asked to see her on his deathbed. He wanted to tell her something. It was this: Who are you to imagine your beauty and talent can save you? It won't be long, believe me, before all that is gone. All that. The truth is what you see here, my body, dying, ugly. A parting gift. Your inheritance. Kiss me good-bye. Notice the color of my teeth, the texture of my flesh. I am gray-skinned.

In fact, says Magdalene, her father, dying, was still beautiful. Only his bitter heart was the color and shape of darkness.

What does a woman want was never the question. It was where does she go in the afternoons. To the shops, to the movies, to the devil, to a cocktail bar. She comes and goes, goes—and comes? Ticking, tocking. Magdalene said: Well, I should let you write what you really think about me. Shouldn't I? I said nothing, holding my breath. Is it—was it—all I wanted? To belong to her in that way? Her fingers drummed upon my bare shoulder. I read aloud to her, caressing her with another phrase, and another. Yes, she sighed. Yes, but . . . yes.

When darkness fell, I left her sighing like the sea, ringing in my shellfish ear.

In my dreams S. Z. Hroch watches me with a quizzical expression.

I write faster, inflicting pain upon my poor subject, smiting her with disease, loss of power, recurring death. Each man loves the thing he kills, I write. No apology to O. Wilde.

One night I dreamed that I called S. Z. Hroch and said I would be late. He reproached me. One night I dreamed I called and said I couldn't come. He reproached me. One night I dreamed that I didn't call and didn't come. I breathed the air of his silent reproach, and went to bed with Magdalene, and drank white wine from her mouth.

It is possible, I begin to think, that in the end she will turn out to have been not a woman at all. Only the imagined idea of desired woman, invented to disguise the homoerotic desires of men.

Rummaging among the trunks and boxes of film and paper, jewels and beaded dresses, Grace Craven discovers a sealed metal footlocker, size of a child's bed. What's in here? she says.

Truth serum, says Magdalene lightly. She is holding up a dress made of glass bugles, the color of water, cuffed in white fur like drifts of sea foam, cut very low in back, to bare the gleaming shoulders.

That night Grace, in a fever of excitement, writes to S. Z. Hroch:

> . . . Metal footlocker. Rocky, it's a climate-controlled laboratory, fitted out like one of those old traveling toilet kits, straps and snaps, metal containers. I hear you say, What? What? Yes, well, I've seen some just like these you'll recall where, I imagine? Containers shaped like bullets, marked with the names of—I mean, a bloody great Swiss bank of world-class ejaculate. She says she came by every one honestly. Kisses, diamonds, something to remember. Sperm! No lover ever refused. She calls them viable options. Meaning they could be activated. Historic babies. Certifiable son of a president, senator, prince, attorney general, head of MI5 . . . Check the DNA, she says calmly. Incontrovertible proof of paternity.
>
> Rocky, she's got this notion—activating them, one at a time. All she needs is a willing girl and a turkey baster. Imagine the willing girls standing in line. I

think I already know two. Three. And I've seen the turkey baster.

And no, I'm not joking. Neither is Magdalene.

TELEX: Craven/Medusa/Care Twist

Flying Medusa Thursday week. Don't touch anything.

HROCH

Rob Twist found this message of more than routine interest. It took his wife, Ione, several hours to find a scrap of paper that clarified it. But the copy of Grace Craven's letter about the footlocker, neatly tucked into a notebook, proved interesting to a number of people besides Rob. Ione too had her secrets.

MAGDALENE

Will Hack said, Let's have our champagne up on deck. There's a broken moon in the water; we could try to put it together.

And I still loved him. Double-crossing ratbastard.

He was touching my hair. I moved my head so that I could feel his fingers on my neck, my throat. And for a moment, yes, that moment just before—when I thought, I don't care, I'd still run off with you. Even now. Anywhere—

But wait. Wife never says that line. That's the Other Man's line; faithful family friend who never dared admit . . . It was midnight, I remember. I said, My foot is full of glass splinters. From the damned slipper. He didn't even smile. I remember thinking I should have given it up long before; should have taken up blond waiters who blush and have old posters of me tacked over the queen-size bed.

Still, his fingers were on my neck, and I leaned against them, and suddenly there was my husband, just behind us, nodding his head. And then I was—then I was—a pushover.

The question is whether I can still do what I came here to do, thought I had to come here to do. Tell the world, have the baby—damn them all, they all *owe* me the baby—risk my foolish neck one more time?

The question is what's it worth, my neck? Ladies and germs, ladies and sperms, I offer you Magdalene Redux, Magdalene reborn, redundant, superfluous, excessive, copious, full. Who'll say a million two, give or take?

Go on, pinch me to prove I'm alive. Give me enough money, love to *prove* it. Once and for all.

Or, how about this for an opening line: Officer, that's him! That's the guy who stole my husband; that's the husband who stole my lover! That's them; I'm positive! Either way, not a bad line, is it? Never been used.

I can just make out Willie Hack's little red racing car. With its little red riding hood that blew up with my poor husband in it. What are the odds on *that* happening two weeks after I jumped or fell?

Broken moon in the water? There was no moon at all. Oh, my poor regrets. I should have sent them. The Magdalene regrets she's unable—

Well, but how would Dietrich have played it? You, there, in the red car! Driving away fast, crossing that bridge when you come to it. No need to signal, just U turn. And I don't want to know your name.

Did you ever love me at all, Willie Hack? As in want to run your tongue slowly over the hidden floss silk that tastes of sea? Sorry at all to have left me like this? Alive, like this?

Good old nepenthe goes to where it does the most good. Here's to me. To the tree that falls in the forest.

Actually it's not so bad now, one grows used to it. Almost a natural stroke, now. The thing one hates the most about one's life, when young, comes back later, not much changed, and suddenly it seems right, comfortable, fine. I am finally what they forced me to become, and now, I see, by God, they were onto something.

Willie, listen, it was probably just your voice. Or the way your hair grows, straight and thick as a boy's, and the color of it. Demerara. The other thing was your fear. I understood it. With other men, I only understood it until I found out who scared them.

And you, but you, I thought.

You're here somewhere, hiding behind it. Fear of me, alive. I could touch you, electricity leaping in my fingers. *Médusée.*

The signs were unmistakable: Grace Craven was growing restless. Magdalene might not know why, but why was never what Magdalene needed to know.

The fact was that Grace's morning excursions into town were nearly as long now as her evening stops at the bar. At first there were breathless explanations; when Magdalene ceased to respond in any way, these gradually stopped. Soon Grace was simply not always there.

One day Grace blurted: Aren't you stifling up here? I can't breathe. We could take a boat to another island—see some ruins—

Other than me, you mean? said Magdalene. But she laughed lightly, and lightly urged Grace to go . . . Consult oracles. Contemplate broken pediments.

Magdalene imagined Grace sailing away with Willie Hack. Stopping in the center of a hot, white street. Whispering I'm *starved;* or If we don't go to bed this minute, *I'll die.*

Panic seized Magdalene's throat, like thirst. The sun blazed. Grace Craven would be far from this balcony, smiling, drinking cool wine. Having left some last chapter of Magdalene's life dangling here like a severed arm. Willie Hack would leap like a child at the sudden turn of Grace Craven's head, as the movement of her mouth silently formed the words: *I'll die.*

The harbor square would be filled with tourists and shopkeepers scurrying to their urgencies. I'll *die,* Grace whispers again, fervently, as they run laughing into a side street; a small hotel sits brooding stonily amid a litter of cheap storefronts. Souvenirs; postcards. Here! says Grace. They stumble out of the whiteness into a dank lobby; shiny, wood-colored wallpaper; faded red carpet. Grace Craven hangs back suddenly, while Willie Hack, in mirrored shades, approaches the high marble desk. A brisk woman clerk, festooned with three pairs of spectacles on elastic bands, presides. We need, says Will, in his beautiful voice. My wife and I . . . Grace has vanished. The clerk scowls at Willie. A room, he says. For the night? Night? he echoes, flushing. She pushes a key toward him; he pushes money toward her, signs the register, turns; Grace emerges from a telephone booth, her smile radiant with naughtiness. Magdalene, she says, sends love.

The room is only a little worse than one might think. View of stray cats, smell of disinfectant. There is an old television set. Willie snaps it on. Life is, as always, three shades bluer than blue. Grace Craven runs to the bed, laughing, peeling off shiny gold spread, blankets, fuzz-coated, plastic, the sort that cannot fold or burn. The sheets are easy care, like Grace. She is between them. Willie fiddles with the TV color; bluer still. Grace laughs again, gently now. Look, says Willie, it's Magdalene, playing a Chinese girl. Her eyelids are taped.

Grace arches backward against the bouncing rubber pillow. Come, she says, tell me a Magdalene story. Show me.

Willie Hack tells her, shows her . . . some of what he knows. Their movements are slow, blue-white, underwater, shimmering and balletic. She moves about him like a manatee, her transparent limbs waving, setting things in motion, though the rest of her remains fixed, rooted to the floor of the sea. . . .

Pink and sparkling, they sail out into the gathering dusk, racing for the last ferry.

She climbs my hill in bounding leaps, like a bank robber after an easy heist. She snaps on the light over the worktable; the piece of my life she left still hangs there like a bit of blue from the sky of an old warped puzzle. It bears the strange look of a distant poor relative, one she is at a loss to place.

There's nothing to drink here, she announces, sulkily, in the doorway. Nothing to eat either, for that matter. I'm *starved*. . . .

Magdalene? Grace is saying. It'll do us good.

What?

A swim, didn't you hear me?

You go, sighed Magdalene.

Grace knelt beside her. Please, she said.

Magdalene turned away. Actually, she said, I'm expecting company.

What company? You never—

Only Ione, said Magdalene. Asked to bring Myrrha, Pollexfen's wife. Can't think why I said yes, but I did.

Ah. Well, then. Grace was wrapping a towel around her bathing suit.

New? said Magdalene.

What, this? laughed Grace. And she was gone.

It was important to swim off the rocks that were preferred by those who were preferred. On what basis the chosen chose their location remained a secret; if you had to ask why here, rather than, say, over there, you did not deserve to swim among Them.

It never ceases to confound some people that others can —indeed, must—create a class system, an impenetrable hierarchical code, within the smallest and most desolate spaces: prison cell, airplane cabin, café table. Who will speak first, to whom? Who will sit beside the newcomer? Which of them will smile, the seeker of favor or the grantor? What will the smile mean? Who will witness it, and how will it be interpreted? Now, here, on this tight island, one sought out the proper rock, and did not climb it unless invited by someone whose striped towel was already spread upon it like a conqueror's flag.

Grace Craven knew all this instinctively; she had learned it, she would tell you, in the second grade, while other children practiced their penmanship, seeking to release the wrist in order to make a looser, more perfect rainbow; a number-2-pencil-thin arc whose every stroke began and ended in a sharp point, always the same sharp point as the stroke before. Other children, Grace said, never looked up from their pages of imperfect, smudged, pointless arcs to meet the gazes of their peers. By the age of seven, Grace had learned those gazes by heart, knew that if they should chance to light upon her it would mean that she had been selected for random persecution, for death by freezing. Grace Craven had never been caught looking up.

Needless to say, Grace had been invited to the best swimming cove. It was, of course, no different from any other: a couple of flat rocks, a sheer drop into the sea, relatively free from jutting points, even for a mediocre diver. Terry Mould and his film crew were already there —pale, English, floppy-hatted, red-nosed, armed with protective sun cream and bathing caps. The poet-novelist was there too, salty and golden-thighed as an old life-guard. And emerging from the sea, a nut-brown naiad, laughing, bare-breasted, glorious.

Who is that? said Grace. Terry Mould laughed. You haven't met Rob Twist's daughter? Name's Hero. Doesn't speak English. I don't mean she can't. She merely doesn't.

Hero rose up: Botticelli's Venus, wearing bubbles of foam like transparent scattered pearls. She wore nothing else, and she wore it as a child does: with not the slightest doubt. How describe her flesh? Smooth, flawless except for the scarred back. But never mind. If she had existed in a Terry Mould photograph, one would sneer that he achieved her with filters, fluid, airbrush. If she were painted by the besotted Tarik, one would wink. Well, obviously, one would say. She was what very young men call a killer, meaning a girl with no notion of her beauty, and therefore no responsibility for its effect upon others.

Wedekind's Lulu, as played by Louise Brooks. Laughing, she rose up out of the foam, shaking her streaming hair. Someone tossed her a ragged towel. She wound it fetchingly about her head. Of course: what else would she think to cover? Terry Mould was introducing Grace Craven to the others. Hero's eyes were closed; she had stretched out upon the rock to dry. *Kahli mera,* she murmured. Good morning.

Terry Mould stood up, yawning; so did the rest of his party, stripping off hats, shirts, glasses; hitching up shorts, snapping elastics. Like a flock of rumpled, skinny-legged white birds, they dove or jumped, shouting, flailing. Hero lay still as a sacrifice.

Mould turned back to shout at Grace. Solicitous. Quite safe here, this time of day, he said. She nodded. All right, then? Up and over!

She hesitated. The others turned to stare. She leapt, then; the water stung, icy, like an angry slap. She began to swim, hard and fast, thinking suddenly of Magdalene, swimming for her life. Magdalene, drowning. Magdalene, stung by the *méduse*. Swimming hard and fast, Grace imagined. Fleeing toward the Peloponnese, shimmering out there, who knew how far? Distances are deceptive; objects on the horizon are always farther away than they appear, the very opposite of objects glimpsed in rear-view mirrors, like one's past. . . .

Still, Grace thought, one could be elsewhere in three days, a week—exhausted, elated, free. They would all be stunned, these people, standing on their chosen rock, shielding squinted eyes, craning sunburnt necks, murmuring excitedly: Can you still see her? I think—there, look, my God, what a champion! Grace Craven! Had you any idea? They would shake their heads, dazed, astonished. No idea.

Grace stopped swimming and looked back. No one had been watching. Hero was still spread out upon her black slab, naked, brown, spangled with sea drops. Still murmuring: *Kahli mera,* Good morning.

Terry Mould's crew has set up a screen and a projector at the bar, so that everyone can see Terry's latest unreleased film. It's the one he did about Kizlar, which the government suppressed after the sultan complained to the ambassador. That Mould. Probing too deeply again. In the old days, Terry said, the complaint alone would have won him every award in England. Sunday supplements would have put him on the cover, surrounded by naked starving children, bleeding corpses, bombed-out ruins. Even in America, Mould via satellite, in ragged safari fatigues, beads of earnest reportorial sweat, explaining who and where, pondering the unknowable why.

Well, the old days. Now, Mould sighed, being a deep prober merely got you deported, if not taken hostage. And at home, merely demoted, if not disappeared.

At Rob's bar on Medusa, people rolled their eyes, professing *déjà vu.* But in fact they were all impressed by Terry Mould. Besides, one never knew what someone like that might still be able to do for one, somewhere, sometime. It's one of the mysteries about islands. Each new arrival thinks one of the others must have the key to some distant kingdom hidden about their person, smuggled in with the carry-on luggage.

Mould himself, cutting his losses, sized up his audience at Rob's bar. Grace Craven must know people? Some backer for his Magdalene, at least? His Magdalene-less Magdalene.

The film rolled. Images of naked starving children, Mould in ragged safari fatigues . . .

Pollexfen there when you were? Rob Twist asked, proffering vermouth-cassis refills.

Terry nodded. One hears the missus will do the chintz and arty bits for the sultan's new palace. Hundred million, give or take.

Myrrha Pollexfen? said Grace. She's a decorator? I thought she was some kind of healer. Orphic, wasn't it? Formerly some kind of terrorist.

Diversification, said Terry. It's a tax thing. But who among us cares about Kizlar? He lifted his glass to the earnest, sweating, deeply probing fellow on the screen. And by the way, he added, winking at Grace, there's no such thing as a former terrorist.

. . . Kizlar is not sexy, his wife, Valerie, was saying. She pronounced the word "sexy" as if it had been an unpleasant surprise in her mouth, like a piece of gristle, discreetly spat.

Ethiopia wasn't sexy, Grace Craven observed. Nor Biafra, as I recall. Takes a single bold piece of film. One clear voice.

Well, Terry sighed, spreading his hands, beaming a modest smile, as though she had complimented him.

Grace nodded back, respectfully, on behalf of America. Public TV, perhaps? she murmured. Terry made the sort of face one makes when controlling a sneer.

It was time to admire the sunset.

Halfway up the hill, in the dark, Grace remembered that Magdalene had been expecting visitors—Myrrha Pollexfen. Sultan's palace. Orphic center. No such thing . . . as a former terrorist.

MAGDALENE

They tell me Dietrich had days like this, suddenly thinking perhaps she was still—perhaps it wasn't over. Foolish, like me, overdosing on the old adjectives, in new voices. Pets fed on rich table scraps. Of course it spoils the animal. Of course it stunts the growth. How else would you train a bitch goddess to sit on your lap? Brain cells destroyed by gentle stroking. Not one ever bites the slow, killing hand.

If by some terrible accident I grow very old, still guarding my tiny treasures, they'll send some pretty young man over, every holiday, with a turkey. And orders to watch me eat it. Not to let me choke on the stuffing until I've signed over everything that's coming to them. Last of the kind masters gets to put me down. Poor fellows. How unfair it seems to them, the waiting.

Bunch of Pygmalions. Waiting for Galatea to turn back into a statue. You think *she* went quietly? Just because some chiseler saw she was worth more dead than alive? Don't move! he said. I adore you when you don't move.

Well, I might still settle for being adored. I do adore it. Even God likes it. He's got it written in his contract.

Of course God's a great judge of adorers. I imagine, by now, he's learned not to trust the ones who bring the turkey.

Someone was at the door. Magdalene waited calmly, twisting this way and that, sifting through what was left of her good angles: moonlit profile, three-quarters, full. Who's there? Not Willie Hack. Never again Willie Hack.

Disappointed? Grace Craven's smile was brighter than the celestial black-and-silver display that Magdalene had just eclipsed. Come in, Magdalene said. I was just—

—have to go in a little while, Hroch's boat is due—but I wanted—

Magdalene turned to avoid the explanation. Grace fell silent, following her to the edge of the balcony. How beautiful it is just now, in the silence, she said.

Magdalene sighed. The woman had come to make love to her, on her way to someone else. Why not get on with it? Wordlessly she drifted inside, arranged herself upon a white muslin sofa, arching backward, raising her face carefully, as if it were an extravagant gift damaged in the mail. Grace knelt and kissed her with unexpected authority. Magdalene liked that, being taken by surprise. She allowed herself to elongate, to assume a languid odalisque pose. Grace's breath quickened; her hands glided like beautiful swimmers. In a moment Magdalene was silvered in the light, covered with Grace Craven's body, and her sweet mouth, her cool whispering voice saying, Beautiful, so beautiful, the line of you from there to there.

Magdalene swam to her, and away, and back again. But she did not speak. It was for the other to say things, wonderful things. Why else make love to Magdalene? Why else would Magdalene love it so?

Grace Craven, spent and glistening like halved fruit, withdrew slowly. They would drink the last of the brandy now, Grace would want to talk, the way women do at such times. Want to tell about the evening at Rob's, about Hroch coming. Magdalene's eyes would half-close like jalousies, as though she were transported, as though cataclysm were still occurring. Perhaps it was.

Grace Craven's eyes shone in the dark; her voice was high and bright, like that of a favored child. She prattled: . . . if I were to publish my own diary? Would you mind? Terry Mould, photographing us together? Oh, and Hroch says the museum won't bid after all, unless you include the loaded footlocker—

Clever stick, sliding it in that way. Magdalene refrained from saying so. But she knew, suddenly, that she had other plans. For the contents of that footlocker; for herself. Though she was—as Grace Craven would say—*starved,* it was a hunger, a ravening, for something other than what Grace, what they all, had thought would suffice. Other than love or money. Attention must be paid, yes. But the price, like Magdalene, had risen.

Grace Craven descends to the harbor to meet the ferry with S. Z. Hroch on it. Coming to discuss this difficult pass they have come to. Not a pretty pass. An impasse.

Until Magdalene is dead—certifiably, no more popping up—the trustees' position is firm. But, darling Grace, what sort of terrible thing is this woman now threatening?

He will kiss her while he says this.

This woman? Grace will say sweetly, after the kiss. Well, my darling, you wanted the goods. And I have found them, in footlockers!

Well, but of course she is not serious, about—

Oh, she is. Yes indeed. One at a time. Unless there's an unexpected demand for more.

Hroch cannot fathom why Grace should seem so—what? he was almost going to think—excited. Until he realized it must be for him, that smile. She'd missed him. Happy to have him here, whatever the mess. Women were like that. He smiled back, as tenderly as he could. She took him to the hotel where she was no longer staying. He carried only a briefcase made of ebonized walnut, like a piece of fine furniture, fitted with locks and invisible hinges, a little funeral casket of a briefcase.

I'll leave you then? she said. Pick you up in an hour, Rob Twist has asked us to dinner.

Oh, he said, startled. Then you're not staying—

I thought, she said smoothly, better if we seemed not quite so together. Considering the delicate moment. Actually I'm up at Magdalene's mostly, anyway.

I see? Hroch said, adding two and two. Well, in any case, darling child, you'll be able to produce a vial or two for me. She's willing, I presume, to have the—stuff—verified?

I'm not sure—

—because we won't be able to go on at all without that.

If you, I assume you still? want to be involved. As broker, that is. Pollexfen wanted me to make that very clear.

Seed money, as it were?

He forced a smile.

Well, it is funny. Live Magdalene worth nothing, dead men telling tales that are worth—what? Millions?

Mm, said Hroch, nibbling her ear. See you in an hour, darling.

Ione Twist, an apparition in black, is streaming down Sea-Squirt Lane. Hair flying, face white and luminous around the terrifying shadows of her eyes. Ione rarely has guests for dinner; she is certain they will never find the house; she has forgotten to tell them the color of the house just below it; Rob has already shouted at her: his grandmother's tablecloth will be ruined by dripping green candle wax, and the cloth is all he has now, apart from the bar, his unfortunate family, and his desperation.

Grace Craven arrives, swathed in pale silk, with the great museum director safely in tow. Hroch is determined to enjoy the evening. He never enjoys such evenings; it is pointless for Grace to remind him of that, or even to sigh.

It begins well enough. The Canadian poet thrusts a poem into Hroch's hand—an assaultive gesture. Hroch reads a line aloud: "The Magdalene is a prick." Reminds me a little of Homer, Hroch says, straight-faced. Wasn't it Homer who called Atlantis an umbilicus?

Rob Twist breaks into huge laughter. Hroch is going to have fun after all. Unless the laughter is another assault. Ione isn't sure; she clatters plates in the kitchen to cover the moment.

Over the fireplace mantel hangs a lovely portrait of two little girls. Painted years ago by Tarik Pailthorpe. Grace Craven stares at it, a classic anachronism, a visual shock against the sun-washed, reverberating whiteness, like Louis Quinze museum chairs in a stark futurist space fantasy. The subjects, all tumbling golden curls, hair ribbons, little rosy pouts. The background somber and rich; tapestried birds, velvet, flowers. The strokes were old-masterly; the artist had been joking. Do you like it? Ione said. Grace nodded. Is his work still like this? Ione shrugged. Nothing is still like this.

One could imagine the young Ione Twist's London dream: rose-colored drawing room, silver teapot. Fragile daughters in sashed lawn frocks, violet-sprigged. Rob Twist had never meant to give her that. One could imagine young Rob Twist's Medusa dream, barefoot, vermouth cassis, sunset, Casablanca. Neither had won. English daughters in shimmering dresses hung like a reproach over this mantel, rendered by the dead-romantic hand of Tarik Pailthorpe. Girls who would have been loved by Lewis Carroll. Who would not run wild, cursing in Greek, bearing the cicatrices of fallen mermaids.

We do go home to England at Christmas, Ione said. Emphasis on the word "home." Next year the girls will start proper school. Grace nodded. Ione's cheeks were striped with violent rouge, as though she had already been struck.

So, Rob says, topping Hroch's drink, unasked. The Magdalene business.

Hroch looks at him blankly.

Rob persists. Pollexfen's not bidding, then?

The museum, says Hroch carefully, has expressed interest. Depending on the—Dr. Craven's assessment of the collection. He moves toward Grace, who is gazing raptly at a wilted blonde woman. Dressage! Grace is saying. Not for years of course, and only just a bit, when I was a kid. She said this in the shy, offhand tone of all her easiest lies. Hroch inhaled sharply. Disapproval? Envy? Dressage! She breathed the word as though she were astride, leaping. Transformed before his eyes into a centaur. Valerie Mould's wary pink-rimmed eyes glowed with sudden pleasure. Hroch suppressed a smile. English. Of course; a horsewoman. Grace Craven had sniffed the saddle soap on her psyche. A woman who, like Hroch's wife, had married down. Dressage? He glanced at Grace. Shameless. How could he reproach her, though, even with a glance. How could he grudge her audacity, seducing the likes of a Valerie Mould, just because she could. As she had him. Dressage? Dubrovnik? Hroch shivered; his sweat was suddenly cold.

Someone said Myrrha had opened her Orphic clinic. Orphic? Hroch went back to Rob Twist. You've seen Magdalene, then? he said. How is she?

Better, I'd say. Although— Rob waited for directional signals.

Pretty bad sting, was it?

Rob nodded; still waiting.

They often relapse, don't they? Weeks, even a month later.

Often, yes.

My guess is she's dying.

Pollexfen's guess? Pollexfen's money on it? Hroch grimaces. Would you like more of anything? chirps Ione. She has forgotten to serve the bread and salad. Green candle wax drips on the ancestral cloth. Ione looks furtively at her husband, but his deepening scowl seems not to be caused by her failures.

The poet offers another poem. An ithyphallic, he explains. Grace exchanges nods with Hroch. I've had enough of everything, Hroch says. Delightful. His tone almost passes for polite.—Long journey, he adds, however, for good measure.

Dead Magdalene, Rob is thinking, pays double. Possibly triple.

After they had all left, Rob sat stonily watching his wife clean up. He could see she was frightened. He could with effort kiss the moist nape of her neck, slide an arm about the thickening waist, avert his gaze. It helped if she was standing over a sink full of steaming dishes. He could feel sordid then. Free to go then, leaving the steam, the dishes, the woman, in their discontent. Cold and full of debt. And somehow arousing for all that. He could not stay to console her just now. She was better left disconsolate. Outside, in the cold, he gulped the dangerous midnight air of refusal, of escape. She was safely inside, hating him for going. He could feel it in his footsteps, higher and lighter as they led him away in the dark, toward the bar. Thief, murderer! She was already behind him, crying over spilled promises. He began to run, for his life.

. . .

S. Z. Hroch was pacing—wait-for-Gracing, he called it—in his filthy hotel room. At 3 a.m. she sauntered in. Magdalene won't see you, she said, in a weary voice, kicking off her sandals. Believe me, she said, I tried every tactic you could possibly imagine. I even said—forgive me—that you'd brought a suitcase full of cash from Pollexfen. She said that with a sidelong glance at Hroch's briefcase, standing there handily beside the bed. Then she glanced quickly at Hroch. You didn't, though, did you, Rocky?

Hroch didn't answer, but made a cage of his hands and pinned Grace Craven to the cold stone wall. The silk gauze slid off her easily, like a skin. She was giggling. Is this passion, Rocky? she gasped. Do you still?

He pulled her down to the floor, none too clean, and they commenced to roll. He had her laughing and gasping, soundless as the heroine in a one-reeler, tied to the tracks.

After a while they moved to the bed. Would you ever, she said, take a place in Tunisia for the winter? Would you ever fly to Marseilles with me, just for a weekend, just to taste the bouillabaisse?

Hroch groaned. Could she still talk anyone—him?—into anything? Even after one had learned the lesson. By heart. How many leaps into the sea? The thing about siren songs is that the tune has infinite variations. The siren parts her hair on the other side, or turns the other cheek, or the rock—the Hroch!—on which she seats herself has a different shape. It now seems somehow . . . solid. Ruddy with sun. Silver with moonshine. It's taken S. Z. Hroch so long, so many busted skiffs, to master all the variations, the entire musical scale, the verses, styles of hair, of smiles, colors of light in the eyes, shape of each treacherous boulder looming in the sunset.

Irresistible, still, because she still believed it.

Choices, she said then, warning him. She would go off with someone else, even someone who trembled kissing her, rather than go on with his (with *his!*) shadowboxing. With *his* now you see me, now you don't. Grace Craven would never admit that she does the same—did it in the midst of her marriage, at the height of the orgy. Admit that for her the tension *is* the attraction. The slippery grasp that forces the cool hand.

Heat of anger, cold blood of acquisitive pleasure, Grace Craven fits in anywhere, like an army of occupation. She makes the very best love on a stranger's floor, and calls it passion, for want of a better name.

Was Hroch back in love with her that night? Pink, damp-haired, mouth the shape and color of a bruised lilac rose, smile a little loose, slightly unsteady on her feet? You bet.

Surprised that I showed up? she asked.

No. Surprised that I did? he shot back.

Well, she said, I rigged that, didn't I? Telling you about the footlocker.

About that—

Ah, yes, I brought you this, she said. Miniature fridge containing three sealed metal bullets. One, the senator, she said. Two, the sultan of Kizlar—father of the present one, I presume. The third one was marked "Old Blue-Eyes."

She watched him tuck the thing into the ice-cube compartment of his minibar.

Sure you'll be able to mix and match?

You did tell her, he said carefully, that we'd do the deal only if this material goes with it? And if it contains what you say—she says. You did tell her that's why I came all this way?

Mm, said Grace, licking him with a pointed tongue. Magdalene wasn't impressed, though.

Why all of a sudden not? He pushed Grace far enough away to study her innocent eyes.

Better offer, I suppose, she murmured.

Suppose?

Fairly sure. Double what we, what I, originally asked you guys for. Without the footlockers, actually.

Bullshit, Hroch said quietly. Who? When? *Texas?* Bullshit.

She shrugged her naked shoulder. I think, she said, that Magdalene is working through another agent. That she doesn't really trust me. Me and you. Pollexfen and me and you.

Hroch thought about that for a minute. What the hell, he thought. Then he said, As it happens, I do have some cash. If she'll see me, if she's willing to listen at all—

She's not, said Grace. How much cash.

Which was when S. Z. Hroch knew for certain that Grace Craven was doing Magdalene in more ways than one. How much cash, he said, would impress you—and/or her?

Grace never answered that. They slept awhile. He made love to her sleeping. Then he whispered what he had to say, as if it were sweet nothing. He told her what he'd told her before. What he'd told Rob Twist. The truth. No point in any deal with Magdalene, except for the footlockers. Until she's good and dead. Buried in immortal prose. With pictures.

What's the cash for, then? she murmured, in her wet, pink sleep. Other business, said Hroch. Magdalene's not the only—

—starfish in the sea? So, Pollexfen wasn't indicted, and you're the new freedom-democracy errand boy. Oh, Rocky.

My ass, he said, unlike yours, is on the line. And he turned her over to make the point.

At nine S. Z. Hroch paid his hotel bill, delivered his cash to the parties for whom it was intended, and caught the first morning ferry. Dr. Grace Craven was still in his bed. For she was, he was here to tell you, a jolly good research fellow.

A game girl with a game plan, and all was fair. She dipped in and out of love and ambition as though it were a honey-mustard sauce. Piquant, she was. Even a soupçon of anger could be used to transform the most ordinary dish of seduction and betrayal into a perfect soufflé of righteous self-defense. High and light, she was; crusty on top.

Well, he thought, she could go on testing her powers; no one would stay long at the center of her. He was—perhaps he had always known it—nothing more than a passing no one. Even when he had first loved her, had she not gone on testing, in the same way, every chance she got? Aha, but she was also married then, and so was he; a fine point. Married, a woman may test, yet not be tested. Ex-married, the bet is off.

So now, exerting her charm on Magdalene, she would

keep old Hroch informed, even to their pillow talk about him. Such a game of girls' rules, leading the chase. Such a dance. By now she should know that S. Z. Hroch does not chase, but cuts and covers. Does not dance, but choreographs.

Do you really want me, Rocky? she once challenged him. Or do you just want to do it to me? Want not, he had replied. Only want not. The response he had learned at four, when his mother died. The stubborn closing of the hungry mouth. He simply refuses to eat, his schoolmasters reported to his father, in writing. He refuses simply.

But that was long ago. Hroch's refusals had grown more complex, more refined. But they sprang from the same despair. Food was not love. He was what he could not swallow.

And Grace Craven would rise from his bed, turning over in her mind what it all might mean, might not mean. Where she must go from here.

See what you've done! Magdalene shouted. Grace Craven was dreaming. Magdalene's voice shattered the silent air of the dream, which was white-gold and cloudless, at the edge of a cliff, high above a phosphorescent rolling sea.

Stop! Thief! Whore! Magdalene shrieked. Stole my—

Grace rolled, sweating and shaking, to S. Z. Hroch's side of the bed. The scream continued. Stole my— and Magdalene's hand, something glittering, flew out in a swinging backhand arc. Grace stumbled and fell, slipping in blood. Then behind her a sudden explosion, shot, car backfiring, mechanical scream blending with Magdalene's, and Grace lay frozen in a fetal curl, face covered in blood. Car? she thought wildly. Drive the car off the cliff? She imagined it rolling, spinning in a perfect slow-motion somersault, like a movie stunt drive. No! Grace cried aloud. She wouldn't! I would sooner than she would, and I wouldn't.

The image, somersaulting car, was still shimmering when the horn started bleating, one high endless note, like a great dying beast. Grace scrambled to her feet and down the hill. Magdalene had driven through an old shepherd's fence. What was left of the car pointed straight up, toward the cliff, like an accusing finger. The fence, demolished, hung in splinters from its ancient hinge. Magdalene, alive, grinning sheepishly. Her bloodied hands thrust through the smashed windscreen. The car horn still bleating: *See what you've done!*

Grace woke up, touched her face, examined her trembling fingers, the damp bed, the empty room. No blood. No Magdalene. No Hroch.

Rob Twist perches on the edge of his daughter's bed. His eyes reproach everyone for unspecified crimes. He bends over the girl, whispering passionately as though they are natural allies, fellow prisoners, victims; as though he must shield her from her mother and other marauding strangers, as though she is still a child, and not, in fact, pregnant.

Hero does not favor him with a reply, not even with a movement of the head. Her mother watches them silently, reflecting. I reared two daughters, she thinks, in my misguided certainty that love prevails, that what I felt was either love or the willingness to love. Arrogance too, I admit the arrogance. What I can't admit is that she is fourteen years old, a child with child, who will not say who the father is. The father, she says, which art in Heaven. Which at least suggests that it isn't Will Hack. God forgive me, I wish I didn't think it was a dead president.

On Magdalene's balcony Grace Craven sipped the potent Bloody Myrrhas left in the fridge by Magdalene's guests. Potent enough to dull any anger but Magdalene's. They were quarreling. About Hroch and the footlocker, about money and sex; duplicity. Grace protested hotly that she had done the right thing, the only thing. It was for Magdalene's own good. She'd see.

Magdalene answered this in silence.

Finally Grace put down her drink. Magdalene swept inside, firmly locking the door that was never locked. Grace went away, breathing in and out, not looking back to see if there were mirrored eyes watching her descent.

Early the next morning she reappeared bearing sweet, pale grapes, just arrived from the mainland; fresh yogurt; warm baklava—all of Magdalene's favorites. Magdalene's eyes shifted from pleased to unforgiving, and back, a difficult set of maneuvers for her, at best, but especially so now, naked under her blowing violet robe, sleep-eyed, hungry. Grace Craven had the advantage. She pressed. After breakfast Magdalene consented to a walk, halfway down toward the harbor, back to the house. Am I coming in? Grace said softly.

What for?

Whatever, said Grace.

Magdalene considered, wavered, full of distrust. Grace understood that she was to plead.

Please, she said, turning away as Magdalene silently turned the knob of her door.

Magdalene lowered her head, a half inch of assent.

They went in, and to bed, carrying burdens that could not be lifted any other way: You betrayed me/I need/so do I/prove it/I can't/then I can't/and besides/even so. But finally they were inextricably woven, braided, all mouths filled, no questions, no answers. Only the silent sobs of the body, depth-charged. Grace whispered against the curve of Magdalene's shoulder. Grace's hair brushed Magdalene's throat. They swam in concentric circles.

It was mid-afternoon before they recovered, emerging in that confusion of senses that marks the traveler's return. I'm *starved,* said Grace Craven. Magdalene never used her voice in reply, at those moments. In her films she or the lover always lit cigarettes without speaking, to indicate depth of feeling, power of a kiss. If they hurried, one of the tavernas might still feed them. They hurried, Grace chattering, Magdalene still silent. By now Magdalene knew that Grace chattered for the same reason Magdalene kept silent. There is really no smooth way home from that journey, one merely acts as if one has not taken it, and soon, minutes or hours later, the denial is nearly true. Like the labor of childbirth—one may recall it daily, recall that it occurred. Yet one hears it said, knows it to be true, that we forget, almost at once, extreme physical sensations—pain, pleasure, terror. How could we go on, otherwise, knowing they could strike again?

And so, there in the taverna, strong drink again igniting their scented tongues, Magdalene asked an ordinary question and Grace answered carelessly, and it was the wrong question and the wrong answer, and Magdalene's face altered, crumpling into its wounds, and Grace grew as angry as Magdalene had been before. They finished drinking in ominous silence, undoing the day, the passion of an hour before; Magdalene went her way alone, and Grace Craven went hers.

That night at the bar Rob Twist told Grace that Magdalene had been taken on a litter to the harbor infirmary. A relapse, he said. *Méduse* does that. He shrugged.

Grace went down to wait for the tests, for the educated guesses of island doctors and primitive machines.

See what you've done, Magdalene whispered.

It was her only coherent sentence.

Not that the doctors and the machines were any more coherent. Pyemia? Erysipelas? A profoundly poisoned condition of the blood, they said. An acute exalted disorder. Her skin was hot, her pulse quick, her tongue glazed. The mischief might be complicated by bronchitis, pneumonia, a curious headache, a drawing-out of the corners of the mouth, a swelling of the eyelids. The face would seem to be covered with a mask. Intolerance of light, mental disquietude, unnaturally acute hearing, delirium, death.

They riffled through books in which her condition was clearly explained: If this, then that. Unless the other.

Doctor, she made love between two violent fights, followed by spiced wine and a plate of eggs. Now her blood suffuses with vitriol.

They shrugged. Complete rest, a diet of beef tea and milk, enemas of brandy, isolation from sympathetic friends. Recovery is possible.

Or death could occur at any moment.

Grace Craven was surprised to see Will Hack standing beside the bed, holding Magdalene's hand. Rob Twist occupied the other side. Guarding their treasure. Grace started: *Their* treasure?

A specialist had been summoned from the poison research center on Salamis. He was Rob Twist's brother-in-law. Best there is, Rob assured Grace. Confident, spectacled, wavy-haired Dr. Hermes Douris said one could take a chance and move her to the mainland, but he would not advise it. Ione Twist added that she did not believe it was the *méduse* at all, did not in fact believe there ever was such a creature, thought it was a figment of evil imaginations on other islands, seeking to divert the tourists.

Days passed. Magdalene's condition remained unchanged. Grace Craven was afraid. Perhaps it was true, what Magdalene had said, in the dream and then in fact. The same words. Grace pondered that. *My* fault, this, wages of *my* sin? She envied the absent others. Terry Mould suddenly called away on urgent business. Tarik Pailthorpe peacefully swilling gin. Magdalene could hardly blame them. Out of her sight, out of her mind.

Grace Craven's work ceased, and her sleep, all sense of time and purpose. Only the fear was a constant. Only the guilt. And the odd ever-presence of Will Hack and Rob Twist. And then, inexplicably, of Myrrha Pollexfen.

. . .

Magdalene slept and slept, until one day she woke, and they said now she must be kept moving. Grace took her on slow walks; they moved like very old people, always looking down. While Magdalene whispered, over and over again, in this terrible slurred voice, that Grace Craven was the cause, the *méduse,* invisible poison in her blood. Light hurt Magdalene's eyes, walking was hazardous, she could not see the path, people moving beside her, she could not know whether walking might stir the blood so that the poison gushed forth again, secret, silent, leaving no trace. The perfect murder weapon. Her own body turning on her, even now, didn't Grace Craven understand, Magdalene had put her life in Grace's hands, Grace had taken it.

Grace Craven said nothing on those excruciating walks. Keeping her head down too, slowing, slowing her step to Magdalene's. The effort was maddening, walking like that, with that faltering, raging voice in her ear. Once Magdalene glanced up sharply at Grace, startled, as if she had suddenly recognized her. You look, Magdalene cried, like some killer nurse! Grace had no reply. Away from Magdalene, she raced about; she careered, heart pounding, lifting her winged feet, flying up the path like a madwoman. Those same feet whose leaden pace she had measured an hour before. She thought of the famous ballerina married to a paraplegic; dancing faster and faster, furiously leaping into her fifties, sixties, heedless of pain, of her aging body rebelling, insisting that it too be still, finally, still as her motionless love, heeding his silent, anguished call, stay beside me, be with me, be like me, be my still life, be my death.

One day Rob Twist said: Pollexfen's boat. A new one. Myrrha had offered Magdalene a cruise, one week, two, everyone could come along, sea air, work wonders. Oh, yes, cried Grace Craven. Magdalene must go. Her vision would clear; she would come to see that she was well, that Grace Craven had not destroyed her. As for Grace herself, no, no cruise, no thanks, she couldn't possibly. She shuddered, imagining a week, two, locked in Magdalene's furious gaze aboard a ship, manacled, waiting for Magdalene to fall asleep, to look away, to leave off hating Grace Craven.

Magdalene was feeling stronger, wanted to go, even wanted Grace Craven to come too. A holiday, she called it. A holiday! I need, Grace faltered, need some time, to myself . . . she could not finish before Magdalene's anger flared again. Not even this would Grace Craven give her. Not even this, after what Grace had done.

Resolute, Grace put Magdalene on the boat with her new and old friends—Myrrha Pollexfen! Will Hack! Rob and Ione . . . Offering a prayer for Magdalene's rest and recovery, and for her own salvation, she wept when the anchor lifted, the boat slid away. Such a silence in the white air.

When Magdalene had gone, Grace Craven returned to the house and began to work on the Magdalene. That very day, endless hours stretching before her like cats, any one of whom could be taken up and petted, stroked, without a murmur. Any one of whom would yield, warm and pliant, offering Grace Craven a gaze of trust, of absolute permission. She began to work.

Work is safe, Grace thought. Passion is—hazardous to health. Work may challenge the order of things; passion disrupts everything. As for love, romance—a construct, an invention, co-opted, corrupted by its very usefulness. To the lover, to the beloved, to all the world that claims to love a lover. Mourning is the best time for love. Romeo and Juliet. Jesus, Marilyn, Elvis, James Dean, Magdalene.

SABOTEUR

Without the *méduse,* without the murderers, she would still have fled. Into idle despair, alcohol, accidental death. A few escape into madness or religion. In Europe some age gently into character. In America a handful refuse to go; we allow them to transform into grotesques, living death figures.

Early surgery was never a good sign. Beauty falling into the wrong hands. Unless passion destroys it first, cleanly. Those were Magdalene's other choices.

The problem is the nature of woman as art. That is, being an artist whose art is portraying woman. The art itself is a sleight of hand, one of the great lies of the world. In theater a practitioner may go on, feeding on a live host. Duse, in her fifties, with a wooden leg, playing *Hamlet.* But a movie star is three times removed. Someone's image of an image performing an image. Who is the Magdalene under the seventh veil?

We are watching the final moments of *White Lady:* The daddy carries the child home, and says softly, Do you see the Lady now, here in the garden? Yes, says the child, looking at Magdalene. There she is. We see her too, in the white cloak she always wears, beside the tree. . . .

But the last time she appeared, she came to tell the child that she was going away, forever. That was why, in the film, the child ran into the woods, pursuing the Lady, her beloved, imaginary friend. That was why the child was lost.

So now, the little girl, saved, says yes, to her daddy: I see her. There.

I see her too, says the daddy. They embrace. But of course he does not really see Magdalene. He is lying, so that his child will know he loves her. There is no Magdalene. Someday the child will believe that.

This was the happy ending. For Magdalene, it was the only kind.

Pollexfen's boat stopped at Scylla, at Charybdis. Rob Twist telephoned the bar and left messages. Magdalene was improving, the light was strong but she shaded her eyes; hatted—that Mexican hat!—and mirror-shaded as always, she promenaded. Fearless, she swam, ate, drank, slept. She was, he said, fun to be around.

Fun! Always was. Except when she was not.

Magdalene's fury haunted Grace Craven's sleep. *See what you've done,* echoed in the nights. Days she wrote furiously, clutching the poor beginnings of her life of Magdalene, her life of Grace.

At the bar, in the tavernas, she spoke of other things, to

other people. She did not speak of Magdalene. She thought that she would never again speak of Magdalene. The parts of Magdalene's life and her own no longer fit together, except on paper. They had become a warped puzzle, something left too long in heat or rain. Magdalene would mend, Grace thought. That at least.

There was a Telex message from Hroch. Sea water, it said. You've been had.

Grace Craven raced up the hill to Magdalene's empty house. The footlocker was gone. In the place where Grace had last seen it, the night she had stolen the vials for S. Z. Hroch, lay a pile of printed legal forms, dozens of them, in perforated quadruplicate, meticulously filled out, stacked and neatly banded like new bills or stock certificates. A handwritten card stapled to the top bundle. Back soon, it said. With considerable interest: Orpheus.

What? What? Dazed, Grace Craven tore around the tiny rooms, ripping at trunks, boxes, the files she had begun so methodically, all her painstaking, precious inventory. Checking every item. Forty-seven thousand individual documents, bits of paper, film, tape, celluloid. Everything was there. Every single other thing.

Grace's fingers shook as she locked the door. She was dripping wet, shivering in the airless heat; she could scarcely breathe. The following day she would take a ferry and a plane to meet Pollexfen's boat. To confront Magdalene. Betrayer, she would say, shaking her, Judas kisser.

Tarik Pailthorpe, drunken painter of pink children, called out to Grace as she stumbled down the path. Between devil and sweet blue sea? he taunted, seeing her weep as she ran. Grace shook her head yes, and then no. She would not have him think she acknowledged his pickled wisdom. She had no idea what he thought he knew. But he claimed her somehow, with his unanswerable question. And she was not, would not be, his lost soul's mate. Would not lose herself as he did, in drink, flight, failure. Grace Craven takes such comforts lightly, discarding them when they bind. The man's work, she thought, dies of pain. Mine embraces pain, but will never marry it. The distance I keep is hardly safe; it takes all of my strength and will to maintain. But turning on the awful point—between devil and sweet blue sea—one may still stand in the center of an island, even this one, and contemplate the plunge, the abyss, the dark. Magdalene is right, Grace said aloud, to herself. This is not her life. It's mine. She did not turn to meet the painter's eyes.

You'll be back! Tarik shouted, with a solemn wave. His tone seemed magisterial, a judgment, a passing of sentence.

Pollexfen's new yacht was wonderful, in spite of itself. Like the piss-elegant lobby of a refurbished movie palace, its red too plush or its plush too red, and the liveried stewards' teeth whiter than their gloves. A Disney World boat, tricked out for bored potentates—impotentates?—

whose notion of Sardanapalian splendor was foie gras and Kobe beef every night, followed by baccarat in fancy dress.

By the time Grace Craven boarded *Halcyon Days,* she had decided to play it cooler, enjoy the ride, postpone the moment—she smiled at what she was about to say—the moment of truth.

Magdalene was reclining in a deck chair, wrapped in a red blanket, sipping beef tea poured from a squat china pot. Salt breeze lifting her hair. Grace Craven realized this was the way she had always imagined Magdalene, life with Magdalene, life as Magdalene. Dinner in iridescent satin pajamas, making love with a synchronous ocean moving secretly beneath her, giving berth to her, a benison.

How are you, Maggie Delaney? Grace Craven said.

Magdalene tried not to smile. No one else called her that. No one else knows. She herself cannot remember when Grace Craven learned it, whether she had told it freely or Grace coaxed it from her. Hello, she said.

Glad to see me? Grace bent to kiss.

No, said Magdalene, this is a gun I've got in my pocket. But during the laughter, she kissed Grace back.

The boat was full of strangers, picked up for next to nothing at various ports. Not jet set, Will Hack whispered. Jet*sam*. As in flotsam.

Myrrha Pollexfen was no longer aboard. Jumped ship a stop or two ago. Things were heating up at the Orphic center.

Heating up? said Grace. What sort of center is it? I always meant to ask.

Dunno, said Will. Orpheus went to hell and back, but lost the girl in the end. Wasn't it?

Mm. Grace had tuned out. I'm dying to gamble, she said. Is there gambling?

Here. Magdalene came out of her cabin carrying a sleeveless white sweater. For luck, she said, not smiling.

Somewhere, said Grace, I read that all love affairs between women end up in squabbles about clothes and lip gloss.

What do two women *do,* anyway? said Will.

Groom each other, said Magdalene.

Like monkeys?

No, said Grace. For stardom.

Grace Craven put on the "lucky" sweater. A hundred dollars' worth, she said. Half an hour. Magdalene frowned like a disapproving parent. And agreed. A hundred.

Each? Grace amended, giggling at the door of the casino. Roulette! she exclaimed. The romantic click of the wheel, the ring of intense faces above black ties and possibly real jewels. *Faîtes vos jeux.* Like in a Magdalene movie, she murmured, blowing Magdalene a kiss. Magdalene left Grace Craven there with her color high, her head set at an imperious angle, the way she gets when she's faking assurance. Her tiny handful of chips ranged bravely before her like a tray of hors d'oeuvres.

And Magdalene went off to play another game, on deck, with Will Hack.

Half an hour later she went back to the casino. Grace Craven had won and lost and broken even and won again. Her face was afire, her eyes glazed. Like a child riding a runaway carousel horse.

Magdalene touched Grace's bare shoulder, lightly. Grace replied with a furious whisper: I'm *winning*.

I see, said Magdalene. But we agreed—half an hour.

Shh! Grace commanded. The wheel clicked; she lost. Again; again. All of it. Lend me another hundred, will you, she snapped. Without a word Magdalene surrendered a bill. Grace Craven doubled it and rose coolly, abruptly. *There*.

And the two, in their shimmering evening gowns, sauntered to the bar for champagne, to celebrate the night, their reconciliation, if that's what it was; their truce. Or Grace Craven's amazing luck. Then they went back to their separate cabins, parting awkwardly in the corridor. They had not said a word about betrayal. In the night Will Hack came into Magdalene's cabin. She heard him packing or unpacking. She said I need to go out, I have something important to say to Grace Craven. He glanced at her sharply, nodded, checked his watch.

And Magdalene went to Grace, eyes streaming, each braced for the mixed torrent of vitriol each thought the other had coming. They did not disappoint one another; acid rain had collected in the downspouts. Magdalene called Grace Craven the vilest names she could think of. She said that she had been having a wonderful time without Grace; a terrible time because of her. She had been deathly ill, and/or buoyant, full of brave adventure. She dropped exotic place names, bazaar adventures, mysterious symptoms. She strung islands and mishaps together, like cheap beads. Grace had the grace not to ask polite questions. Magdalene said she had been, had been . . .

Grace listened with her head bowed like a penitent under the rain of deserved blows. Deserved? Well, Magdalene thought they were, believed they were. Magdalene was trembling with the righteous force of it. Along the way they both lost track of the crime. Never mind. When the storm abated, Grace said—quietly, carefully—that she had reached a decision. She was through. She would not go on with Magdalene's life.

Magdalene's lip curled. Perfect, she said. The word dripped. Poison fumes rose from it.

I need, Grace said, to go back to my own life. My own—

Of course you do, said Magdalene. Is that all, then?

Which of them reached out? One of them must have. One of them must. They sank to the floor of the cabin in a sudden violent tangle; each claiming some claim, renunciation, denial. Not another word. Only bruising mouthfuls of each other, signifying Yes-no, no-yes, canceling each other out.

There was a sharp knock on the cabin door. Grace Craven glanced at Magdalene. Magdalene glanced at the clock beside her. Three? Four? The pounding, invasive as the cry of a child waking from a nightmare, stopped, then started again, again. How long, how many times, with what urgency? Each of them imagined the visitor half asleep, bewildered, wondering why there was no answer, refusing to know, or to stop, someone must be there, must answer me. Would he break it down, finally, the door, attack them with his stricken eyes? Magdalene and Grace lay breathing into each other, enduring the silence with each other's treachery in it. And his.

At five Magdalene rose and returned to her cabin. Will Hack was stretched out, wrapped in blue-white sheets. His eyes were pale, his face clenched as a fist. Why didn't you answer? he said. Magdalene didn't answer. Why? he demanded, louder. I couldn't, said Magdalene, breaking into tears. I can't. Please.

Can't what? Please what?

Can't anything. Renounce her. Magdalene took to the bed, leaking.

At six Grace Craven burst into Magdalene's cabin, shouting and attacking. Demanding that Magdalene choose, act, decide. Magdalene lay curled in the fetal position. Will Hack, delivered from his anger by Magdalene's watery helplessness, sprang to defend her. She was perfectly fine, he said. She had decided, she was sure. Leave her. Alone.

I? I? shrieked Grace Craven. She came to my cabin. Ask her why. Go on. Ask her.

This was of course unaskable, unanswerable. Touch her there, Magdalene could have said. Or taste the dark corners of her mouth. But Magdalene said nothing. Will Hack made no move, no sound. Grace Craven went out, slamming the door.

Three hours later, at breakfast, Grace regaled those who hadn't been at the gambling tables with the story of her turn at the wheel. She altered the ending only slightly, so that, after Magdalene staked her with the second hundred, she left the table with four. No one quibbled; Grace was the historian.

So what would go on at an Orphic center? one of the new arrivals asked.

Reincarnation, replied Valerie Mould, with a knowing smile.

Oh. Right.

Grace Craven suddenly noticed that Valerie Mould was looking oddly puffy. Pregnant? Why should that make Grace think of Myrrha Pollexfen and the missing footlocker full of . . . How's Terry? she asked brightly. Did he finish his Magdalene?

Valerie Mould looked at her coldly, and changed the subject.

The following day the boat paused for the obligatory afternoon swim. Grace was badly stung on the thigh by a *méduse.* The three of them, Grace, Magdalene, and Will Hack, had been swimming close to shore; the others were on the boat or far out in the water. Grace screamed; only Magdalene and Will heard her.

By now even Magdalene was an old hand at this; by now she knew as well as the natives that the thing to do when *méduse* strikes is apply fresh urine directly to the sting. Willie must do the necessary. Manfully, he stripped off his black bikini. Grace Craven lay on her side, injured thigh up. It was a remarkable thigh; Grace Craven was a remarkable damsel in distress. Magdalene hung back discreetly, considerately, as Will Hack tried to summon his healing balm. He tried and tried; nothing.

Grace Craven, biting her lip, murmured encouragement, little jokes. Magdalene was struck by the tenderness of her tone, coaxing him, like a mother.

Through her pain, her tears, Grace finally laughed, to put him at his ease. Will laughed, too—embarrassed laughter, failed laughter, chagrin. But he could not quite pee on her thigh.

At last she let him off. I'm all right, she gasped, stumbling to her feet. I'm fine, I'll get back in—the water, the salt will help, there's stuff on the boat—and she broke into a run. The thigh was aflame, great splotches of red, swelling, spreading. Will Hack, not looking at Magdalene, hitched up his bikini, ran after Grace, into the sea. Magdalene followed them slowly, at a respectful distance. Will and Magdalene tacitly agreed never to speak of this incident. Grace and Magdalene spoke of it in whispers all that day, finding it signal, hilarious, awful.

On the boat, Will applied the bottled ammonia, expertly, to the stricken limb, rubbing solemnly. By the time the boat pulled into its port for the night, the swelling had subsided, the splashes of crimson paled to shocking pink. Will Hack was silent, on deck in the darkness. All three drank too much wine, obliterating, for the moment, the sharp edge of the unmentionable. The two women drifted away finally, leaving him to regain his dignity. They began to walk slowly, not exactly together.

Grace suddenly said, Where is it?

Magdalene hesitated, as if she could not quite decide

what the question meant. Oh, she said, then. I gave it all away. To a good cause. Actually I'll get a little something back. Possibly a lot of something. She shrugged, Possibly not.

What are you talking about? Grace stopped walking, stationing herself so that Magdalene must stop too. They leaned over the railing. Magdalene finally replied: Myrrha Pollexfen. My executrix. I always liked that word. Sounds like a whore in pinstripes. Little silk bow tie— She giggled.

You gave Myrrha Pollexfen millions of—she's running a *sperm* bank? Famous men's—? Like a dead escort service?

I wouldn't put it that way, Magdalene sighed. I gave the gift of life. Poor infertile women, I mean rich infertile women—who want only to hold, say, a president's son, a sultan's princeling, in their lovin' arms. And where the lady can't bear, say, actually *bear* the little bastard, the center provides a middleman. Middle person?

Womb rentals, she does womb rentals?

Well—

How much, Magdalene? Apiece. So to speak.

Um, I think it's five hundred and up. Five hundred thousand. Depending. And I'm not the only source, you know. Stuff coming in from all sorts of people. Wives, ex-wives, mistresses, one-night stands. Men, too. From all over. Really, it's fabulous, when you think. Myrrha only sent out the one mailing. I lent her my address book. Very good pitch, I thought. Put his money where your mouth is. Half the profits go to green causes, save the rain forests, rhinos, sea turtles, God knows. And of course the Corsican nationalists—

Grace suddenly started. I think Valerie Mould is pregnant.

Yes.

She wouldn't, perchance, be carrying some, other than Terry's . . . genetic material?

Magdalene moved one creamy shoulder. Terry Mould turns out to be a very bad egg. Bad sperm. Trades in kiddie porn. In the Far East. Kiddies doing—you know. Really hard stuff. Not to mention—

Terry *Mould?*

Magdalene snapped open her silver evening purse, and withdrew a small flat packet. Here, she said. His most successful line. Guess who. Someone utterly famous.

Grace held the photographs up to the moon. I can't quite. Shirley Temple. Gloria Jean. Rita—

Well, I'm hurt. You didn't recognize the birthmark on the left—

Grace said nothing, studying each photograph, then handing the packet back. Oh, God, Magdalene.

I was four, Magdalene replied. Terry Mould seems to have excellent contacts.

So Valerie's your avenging angel? With whose sword, may one ask?

Even I don't know. Think of numbered Swiss accounts. Maybe she'll send announcements, though. One can, you see, sue the father's estate for support, inheritance. Rightful heirs to every throne. Illegitimacy's no barrier anymore. Enlightened times.

Grace burst into wild laughter; it seemed somehow the only logical reaction. This could—this is quite some terrorist tactic.

So Myrrha says. Benign takeover of every significant fortune in the so-called civilized world. And not a shot fired in anger.

Ain't you something else, said Grace Craven. And did not ask herself why, considering everything, Magdalene should be trusting her with explosives.

Do you love me a little? she asked instead.

A little, Magdalene conceded. But she was to spend that night alone in her cabin, while Grace Craven lay awake turning over in her mind what it might mean, might not mean, where she must go from here. She must get to a safe phone, she decided at last. Must send a message to Hroch. Saying? That they had *both* been had. And, but, did Pollexfen know what his wife had done to all of them? Could he—in fact—have put her up to it?

Oh, God, she thinks then, sitting bolt upright. That's it. This way the museum acquires the Magdalene for nothing. Deftly cutting Grace Craven out. And Hroch too? Leaving only Magdalene's eventual death to send the collection's value into the multimillions. Assuming he'll wait. Pollexfens don't wait. Which means somebody, bodies, are assigned to take care of that last detail. *Halcyon Days*. Pollexfen's boat. No such thing as a free ride.

Shaking, Grace arose, dressed, went out on deck to smoke. Will Hack was there, muffled in a glorious white vicuña coat, silk scarf blowing. My luck, Grace thought. Should have worn Magdalene's sweater, to match.

MAGDALENE

I can hear them. Voices low, pleasant. They are negotiating. She'll promise to deliver me to him, for a price, her fair share. I knew this. Knew we'd all end up in the same boat, like the other time, three of us, each insisting on rights, promises, love. Bargaining for the life of me. I said yes all the wrong times.

Voices churning softly, like the wake of this boat, so reasonable, soothing. I am like an impossible child put down for her nap, while the grownups decide what's to be done about her.

He'll say he has to do what he has to do. She'll say she needs, she deserves, she's earned. He'll understand. She'll concede. And turn, and turn about. Don't I know this movie? The characters, the clothes, the setting. The dialog hardly varies, there isn't much of it. The plot thickens, thins, twists. It has no denouement, no deus ex machina, no resolution. It's always like this, until suddenly it's like that. And again, just when you think, or even before that, depending on the music. This is comforting, like the soaring theme of *Gone With the Wind,* which marks the station breaks. You are there.

So she'll help him. He'll do right by her. They'll finish their cigarettes, relieved. And now there are three people on this boat who expect to make a killing on the Magdalene. Not counting me.

There was a patch of violent weather; Ione Twist took to her cabin and did not emerge. Rob Twist and Will Hack seemed always together, huddling, speaking in low tones.

Squabbles erupted among the new passengers, at the gaming tables, in the bar. Everyone sulked, in corners, sprawled among their separate strewn piles of damp towels, magazines, rubbish. Magdalene thought of the clusters of grapes, abandoned, ripening in the sun beneath her stone balcony; of the fig tree down the lane, bearing fruit that she will never gather.

Grace Craven stayed up late drinking brandy, watching the storms, imagining harbor lights. Couples of all sorts went to their cabins, divided by the thin partitions of habit and the social order. Some, perhaps, made love. Some listened for neighboring sounds. Some turned toward or away from the designated partner. One said how beautiful and strange it was; how ugly and strange, said another.

In the daytime they rushed in and out, dirtying glasses, flaunting new sweaters; exchanging nods, strained monosyllables, seasickness pills.

Once on Medusa Magdalene had asked Grace what she thought they were doing. Voyaging, Grace had said. Now, voyager, Magdalene said, when they met on the heaving deck.

On the third and worst of the stormy nights, only a handful of stalwarts made it to dinner. Valerie Mould among them, to everyone's surprise. They were talking about movie stars. Valerie said no amount of fame or money ever satisfies them, because *they* are the food.

Yeah, muttered Will Hack. Who was it said they give you a thousand a week until you need it?

One of them, Grace sighed. Tough to be the image of your keeper, in drag. Leonardo's Gioconda. Sternberg's Dietrich. Wilde's Salome. Everybody's Garbo. An icon is just an I, conning.

So just watch the image, said Rob Twist. Never the lady herself. Hand quicker than evil eye. That's how the gods finally got rid of Medusa. Brave Perseus gazed only at the monster in the mirror.

I believe, said Grace Craven, it was a goddess who taught him that trick. And the mirror was *her* shield.

The following morning they awoke to a brilliant, cloudless sky. If the boat had changed course in the night no one noticed. Most of them would not have cared. Most would have gone along for that ride, in any direction. Pollexfen's boat. *Halcyon Days*. Any port in a storm.

MAGDALENE

They won't dare try another suspicious drowning. They're counting on my *méduse*. Another "relapse." The quintessential sting operation. Well, I'm ready, this time. Minute doses of the venom, by eyedropper, as a mithridate. Doing it every day, since they put me in that clinic. Myrrha's idea; Myrrha's stuff. Saved my life once, so far.

When we pull in to port, tomorrow, day after tomorrow, news of my death will be carried ashore. I'll go quietly. Gentle, into that good night.

After that, I haven't a clue. Well, maybe just one.

THE GOSPELS

(FROM THE TAPES, EDITED BY G. CRAVEN)

1. *Twist*

Magdalene died last night, having slipped into a coma, trying at last to speak to us. She had had her toenails polished with a silvery mauve lacquer, and her hair freshly washed with streaks of copper and dull gold, like a dying sun. She was late for dinner. Slipping away, instead, sudden change of plan, very last minute. Leaving early to avoid the rush, willing to skip the final scene, unhappy ending, death of the heroine, inescapable. On the final day of our voyage, I saw her falter once on deck, clutching the rail, keeping her head down, fearful of falling. She whose eyes had so feasted on the rushing world, its panorama of colors and flavors, bursts of sound. She was trying to speak to us, at last, urgently. What could she have meant to say? Surely not that she was sorry not to have cherished any of us. Surely not. Nor that she was going now, finally, to a place where no one would remark on her perfection, where the perfection of a Magdalene is commonplace.

I wonder what Heaven could hold for her, if Heaven has no need for film, no need to record the movement of her flawless face in laughter, the column of her throat, the rustling of her pink-and-silver gown. Is Garbo here? Stanwyck, Gardner, Crawford, Davis? Which of them will speak first, graciously, to the new arrival? How will they behave if none of them makes a scene for the other to admire?

Magdalene died trying to tell us the truth that mattered to her. We are condemned to listen for it. The little house at the edge of a cliff, where she had spent her last desperate exile, is hushed now, somber, asleep in dazzling sun. She had taken to keeping shutters bolted, because, she said, light was cruel.

One by one her treasures had vanished, little silver boxes, a handsome tortoiseshell clock, the lovely Pailthorpe portrait of a girl with red-gold hair and ice-colored eyes, the girl Magdalene had perhaps once meant to be. Sold to dealers for ready cash, to be spent on pitiful things, scarves of not quite silk, copies of fine bracelets she once owned. Things to palliate the horror of shabbiness, lest old admirers avert their eyes or, worse, display the little *frisson* of satisfaction that consoles those who never have far to fall.

It was a brave death, modest, not showy. She plunged headlong, rather than grow smaller, looking down. She made her exit as she always had, from a dazzling white room, the sun dancing on her mirror. Plump white sofas, cream-colored carpets carved in thick furrows; a room that might have come from her earliest films. But all that white, she complained, seemed to have turned yellow, like old people's eyes. On an impulse last month, she had had the walls painted a very dark green; in the late evening, in soft lamplight, with straight gin sipped from an oversized cut-crystal glass, any stranger might still have seen only the elegance, only her mystery. But the harsh noon sun exposed the trick. One flinched for her, standing there, wanting only to protect her, to plead: Magdalene, take my coat. No telling when that gilded clock on the wall stopped; in her life Magdalene made a point of never knowing the time, though she loved clocks, fancy old ones like that, with the fan-shaped pendulum, like a gown of golden lace, and a perfectly smooth face unmarked by the passage of time. . . .

2. *Hack*

Now seems as awful a time as any to recall the death. The final hours, wheeling her on a stretcher out of the clinic, a woman official in a black suit running alongside, crisply reminding us to return the linens.

The taxi ride, around the square to the hotel, required by law. No one gets to carry the dying around the square. Not in that town. And the hired nurse, twenty-four-hour deathbed vigilante, also required by law (lest what?). We signed papers taking full responsibility (for what?) so that the clinic, the island, would be protected (from what?). Death is a public act; we are all at risk. The feeding tube had to be disconnected. Ah, so that is how it's to be, said the nurse, grim as a reaper. The clinic does not permit *that* on the premises, even when they know the person dying has no chance of ever taking another sip of water, another breath on her own. How Magdalene loved the gaiety of dining well. Silver and crystal, fine china edged with brilliant colors. Linens and flowers and beautiful perfumed women, whose shoulders gleamed in candlelight, like hers. Magdalene gave no consent for a feeding tube. Gave no consent to be carted away, kidnapped from our boat in the dead of night (the dead of night!), invaded by insidious devices, held, imprisoned, exposed to harsh light. No consent to incur bills.

Only once can I recall her going to consult a doctor, complaining of mysterious trouble. She was kept waiting an hour in a dreary brown room, surrounded by dour, badly dressed strangers, dusty plants, magazines about dull things. Her visit cost more than a wonderful hat and a splendid luncheon. Lobster, champagne, caviar. No one in that doctor's waiting room could have promised her a dazzling new screen role, a TV cameo, a pretext for any sort of celebration. Magdalene had lived long enough to know when money was wasted. The mysterious trouble was never again mentioned. I don't know if it went away. But in that hour she had in fact found something of value: that not enough relief from terror or loneliness can be purchased from doctors. Women like Magdalene always did better in shops, restaurants. She was broke at the end, but not too broke to resist. And she resisted the doctors that night, succumbing to death but not to them. She wanted to die better than she had lived, her lovely body inviolate at last. We heard her cry, Leave, me, alone.

But they would not. For a night and a day she was their property, she, robbed of her self. Held hostage. We released her, finally, I did, with the help of her closest friends, defying official rage, accusations, legal threats. They surrendered her to us and took away their systems of support.

I stayed in the hotel room while she began to die, her body struggling against itself, choking, groping—she could neither breathe nor swallow, but the memory of breathing, of swallowing, went on—terrifying, the sound of those two primal impulses, letting go, giving up, holding on, yes, no. I knelt sobbing on the floor next to her bed, holding her hand. There was no last word. No love, no farewell, no fuck-you. She just, all of a sudden, wasn't Magdalene.

And yes, I loved her.

3. Mould

I remember the day she came to us, from the sea; it was odd, but somehow we had been expecting her, as though she had promised not to leave us, and we believed her, against all reason. Those of us who knew her as a girl, before artists thought of painting her, photographing her, before hers was the face on the thousand-yttria note, we believed. On Medusa, she seemed the personification of Phryne, the island's patron saint, she who was crucified in her red peasant dress, her crisp white apron, her little black shoes. Phryne's slender arms, daintily pinned to the cross, the cruel wounds decorously covered by white flowing sleeves. Her head bowed modestly, awaiting the release of her sweet soul.

There is no official history of why Phryne met death this way on Medusa. Early engravings suggest that she could not in fact have had a clean apron on at the last moment, since she had just been horribly tortured. Historians also disagree as to whether the good people of Medusa themselves were her executioners, or whether barbarous invaders did it. We can't be certain. We *are* certain that she died on the cross; an Imitatrix, they call her. As if she staged her death to get attention. Perhaps she resisted enemy soldiers, refused to dance their pagan dances. In any case, Phryne's birthday is celebrated on Medusa, with feasting and solemn revelry. Women wear the red dress and white apron, and dance the dance of fate worse than death. Magdalene was their Phryne incarnate; her portrait on the thousand-yttria note showed her in the costume.

So that when she came back, rising out of the sea, Medusa took it as a sign. She had brought the island treasure, as if she herself were not treasure enough. Bearers staggering under their burdens followed her up into the hills, then fell to digging with shovels; half a dozen graves were dug, steamer trunks disappeared. And the bearers left the island on the common ferry, though they had come on another boat, a fishing trawler, white, with a red sail. The vessel disappeared too; no one saw it go.

When was all this? The gossipists' ballpoints were poised like scalpels. Their tape running. Their eyes alight.

Let me think, I said. June? No, January. It was just after the famous suicide, wasn't it? You must remember, the disappearance? the mysterious drowning? It was then. Every detail precisely recalled, the color of the sky, the time of day; everyone remarked the coincidence.

Now, if we can have those lights down, we'll begin my film. Magdalene: Here's looking at you.

SABOTEUR

The old siren died, still rewriting her song. Hair like spun circus sugar, face masked with makeup and drugs, her voice, that voice, a self-parody, which had once been merely a parody of Marilyn's parody of Lana. It is, she said, better not to survive, they charge us too much for the time. Her face was punished not only by the sting of the *méduse,* but by surgeons long before (for having once been perfect? Having never been perfect enough?). It was not the color of a face. Like a piece too long worked on, computer-colorized, tampered with. Whose reflection did she see in the glass she kept confronting, staring rudely, as if it were a prying stranger. Some familiar shadow of Magdalene past? She would have laughed at that, soundlessly, without pleasure. Time will not be bought, she said. Which is why we have to kill it.

I am thinking of her, though, in a long silver robe, embroidered, quilted in fantastic swirling patterns, buttoned with brilliants large as dollar coins. She sat for her portrait in that robe, composed as a queen of heaven, in her white-gold room. I have that portrait still. It is perfectly ordinary, a photograph of a woman in a silvery negligee. But for the child I was when I first saw it, the robe was alight, radiant as the moon. And the woman's white, smooth face, in its halo of illuminated hair, with expressionless eyes that gazed past me toward some worthier thing, was what I thought we meant by God.

She kissed many who could not claim her, assenting only to the obligation of the kiss itself, the moment of it, not the one before or after. How bereft were those who needed, wanted, demanded more of her than that.

When the boat pulled in, champagne was served on deck, passengers leaning over the rails, obligatory photographs, flashes of tiny light, goblets raised to the statue of Phryne in the harbor.

And then in the waiting crowd ashore she saw all the men who ever loved her, standing together, faces upturned, searching for a sign.

She and I said our farewell, slowly drained the last of our champagne, tossed the fragile crystal into the sea.

Magdalene died the following night. They told me when my plane reached New York.

Which is how it always ends—no bang, no whimper. Not the truth of Magdalene, however. Not the secret, the catch, the sleight of hand quicker than the eye. The moment of truth, after all, is only that—sudden flash of accidental clarity, before one quite knows that something is being recorded, by someone, for some reason. Once it escapes into the pen, the brush, camera, micro-cassette; once seen, read, recognized by anyone who may profit from it, no truth is ever again quite so true, quite true enough. Like the beauty of Magdalene, the fame of her pursuers, the folly of those who needed her to believe in. Truth turns out to be just another killer of the thing it loves.

TELEX: S. Z. Hroch, Museum of the Arts

Magdalene collection complete. Come and get it. Trust briefcase holds million two. Each.

Craven, Hack, Twist

For the record, Grace Craven was wrong about the Pollexfens. Ran had not in fact put his wife up to anything. Not even her new pregnancy.

The Orphic center on Medusa was firebombed and picketed by right-to-life groups, feminist lawyers, a coalition of religious sects. The place was finally closed down by mainland authorities, as a hazard to the public safety.

Ran Pollexfen filed divorce proceedings in the States, charging Myrrha with adultery, co-respondent unknown. He plans to remarry, a Rumanian woman rumored to be a former professional escort in Kizlar.

Terry Mould's documentary film *Magdalene* was shown at the Ajaccio Film Festival; several American distributors expressed interest, although some critics were disappointed that there were no actual shots of the star as she looked just before her death.

Rob Twist's bar on Medusa has expanded; the yard has been paved, gleaming restaurant equipment installed. A dozen marble tables with square market umbrellas surround a small pool with a fountain. It looks lovely at night, with all the little white lights in the trees. The daughter had an abortion, after filing some claim against the estate of a prominent senator. The affair was settled out of court, for an undisclosed sum.

Tarik Pailthorpe sold his nude drawings of Magdalene to the Modern, but retained the licensing rights for posters and cards. You can buy these at the harbor shops, at Rob's bar, or from the artist.

Will Hack had just signed a lucrative contract to do a television campaign for a new luxury sports car when he was killed in that midair collision over Nish, between two private jets. The other plane carried twenty-eight passengers, including Valerie Mould and the sultan of Kizlar.

The museum deaccessioned its Magdalene collection for twenty times what it paid. The new film institute at Atlanta has announced plans to house the Magdalene in a special wing, if funding is approved by the federal arts administration. S. Z. Hroch, former director of the New York Museum of the Arts, has already assumed his new post as head of the Atlanta operation.

Grace Craven is completing her work on adultery in postwar film noir. She has declined offers to publish her Magdalene memoir, though she is scheduled to introduce the Magdalene film series again at Rutgers next semester.

. . .

Sightings of Magdalene continue to be reported on various islands in the Aegean, and as far east as Ephesus, on the Turkish coast. Already there are cultists who claim she never died at all, but was assumed, bodily, to heaven. Never assume, Magdalene herself used to say. Only the Virgin had to go that route. Immaculate, immortal—the game has its rules.

A NOTE ON THE TYPE

The text of this book was set in Bembo, a facsimile of a typeface cut by one of the most celebrated goldsmiths of his time, Francesco Griffo, for Aldus Manutius, the Venetian printer, in 1495. The face was named for Pietro Bembo, the author of the small treatise entitled *De Aetna* in which it first appeared. Through the research of Stanley Morison, it is now acknowledged that all old-face type designs up to the time of William Caslon can be traced to the Bembo cut.

The present-day version of Bembo was introduced by the Monotype Corporation, London, in 1929. Sturdy, well balanced, and finely proportioned, Bembo is a face of rare beauty and great legibility in all of its sizes.

Composed by Dix Type Inc., Syracuse, New York
Printed and bound by The Haddon Craftsmen, Inc.,
Scranton, Pennsylvania